SARAH'S
FOOTSTEPS

First Published in Great Britain 2016 by Mirador Publishing

First edition: 2016

Any reference to real names are purely fictional and are constructs of the author. Any offence the references produce is unintentional and in no way reflects the reality of any locations or people involved.

ISBN: 978-1-911473-68-8

Mirador Publishing
10 Greenbrook Terrace
Taunton
Somerset
TA1 1UT

Sarah's Footsteps

Alice Gent

Acknowledgements

Firstly I want to thank my wonderful husband, Sam, for his endless support and love. My mum, for her wonderful ability to iron out plot holes and grammatical errors. My dad for slogging through so many of the epics I wrote as a teenager and finishing every one. My dear friends Bryony McCann, Kit Meeson and Joe Bain for taking the time to fine comb through this story and their insights into the plot. Kate Noseley for helping fill in the details with her testimony. My incredible church family at Emmanuel City Centre for always being so loving. Sarah Luddington for all her hard work getting it published along with the rest of the team at Mirador.

Finally, I would like to thank all those who poured time and prayer into me at University to help me grow exponentially in my faith. And of course, who could deserve more thanks from me than my wonderful Saviour, who deserves the praise for any good found in this book.

Dedication

To all the Izzys of University, and those who are a Fran, an Anna or a Josh who give up so much to fight for them.

'Many have undertaken to draw up an account of the things that have been fulfilled among us, just as they were handed down to us by those who from the first were eyewitnesses and servants of the word. With this in mind, since I myself have carefully investigated everything from the beginning, I too decided to write an orderly account for you, most excellent Theophilus, so that you may know the certainty of the things you have been taught.'

Luke 1: 1-4

"Of The World."

Chapter One

I studied my face closely in the mirror and decided to add another layer of eye shadow. I was becoming proud of my make-up skills, yet nothing I did ever seemed to make my nose less pointy. And then there was that spot on my chin that already had five layers of foundation over it. I finished darkening my eyes, pouted and blew a kiss at myself.

"What do you think?" I asked, whirling around to where Sarah was stretched lazily across my bed. Her eyes flicked up from her phone, taking in the amazing heels, my favourite mini skirt and the translucent lace top.

She half smiled, pushing her straight brown hair away from her face. "You look pretty. I like your hair. Won't you be cold though?"

I snorted at her. "I'll get a beer jacket soon enough. Anyway it's warm in the club." I watched her eyes linger on my top and I knew she didn't approve, but didn't really care. She was so old fashioned and didn't realise how liberating it was to feel all the guys watching you. I wanted to feel sexy enough tonight to attract Tom. Maybe we'd kiss. Maybe he'd invite me back around to his... Looking my best I felt so powerful. She never understood any of that.

I sat down on the bed and smiled down at her, tugging at her jeans. "You should come too, have a laugh."

She smiled in amusement. "It's hardly my scene, is it Izzy. Besides I'm singing at church tomorrow morning. I'll need to get up."

I rolled my eyes. "I'm sure you're allowed one night of fun. Get somebody else to sing." I grabbed her hand. "Come on, Saz, there's more to life than A levels. It'll be fun!"

Sarah sat up and looked me in the face. "Izzy, I like dancing, but not in a hot, cramped hole underground where half the boys are trying to grope you and the girls are stepping on your feet. You'll be after Tom, I'll just get bored." She smiled. "Have fun without me. Beth and Jen will be there, you don't need me."

I stood up and started to pack my clutch from my neatly arranged dresser, sighing at the amount of times we'd had this conversation before. "You know, Saz, if you just lightened up a little and stopped being so boring, you might actually have fun. You just need a few drinks in you."

She screwed up her face. "You know I hate the taste of alcohol."

"Only 'cos you don't try enough to get used to the taste." I gave my face one more look in the mirror, studying each detail. My blonde hair was painstakingly curled and sprayed, every clip in place. My brown eyes seemed to glow under the fake eyelashes. I looked good, I knew that, but if only my nose was smaller, rounder, I would look so much better. A sudden lurch of insecurity hit my stomach, and I turned away, telling myself I was being ridiculous. "I'm ready, take a photo?"

Sarah sat up and rolled her eyes dramatically. "You're so vain," she teased, picking up my phone to take a picture.

I laughed. "Well none of the photos later on will get my shoes. Just look at them, Saz! Look at them and weep."

She giggled and took the photo. "You will be doing the weeping at the end of the night, I think. They're ridiculous!"

I linked my arm through hers and we walked down the stairs. Jack was playing his new Xbox loudly in the sitting room, trying to shoot something. It shot back by the sounds of his swearing at the screen. Through the closed kitchen door, Mum was arguing with Kieran again. I was getting fed up with the drama in the house, with Mum in tears most weeks. I'd sworn long ago that I'd never let men treat me the way they had treated her.

Sarah looked uncomfortable as I shouted through the door that I was leaving. She didn't understand how lucky she was to have parents that were still civil to each other.

"Be safe, honey. Nice to see you, Sarah," shouted back Mum, before resuming her complaints in quieter tones.

It was cold outside and I squished myself into Sarah's cotton jumper for warmth as we hurried to her old car. My heart was beating with excitement. So many things could happen tonight. Tom was going to be there with his mates and I'd been after him for weeks. I pictured his face and imagined kissing his lips, his hands caressing my back. I felt hot and my stomach tightened. What a stir it would cause at school if we dated... *everyone* loved Tom! I'd thought him way out of my league until he'd danced with me three Fridays ago and he'd held me close to him until I'd felt drunk on his masculinity. I hadn't stopped thinking about him since. He was just... perfect.

I half fell into the passenger's seat and glanced at Sarah as she drove, the car clanking noisily every time she changed gear. "Who do you fancy? There must be somebody?"

She shook her head. "Nobody at the moment."

I sighed, exasperated. "Come on, there must be some nice boy at your church or something?" How could she not want to experience the excitement and devoted attention of a boyfriend? The intimacy? The confirmation that we are sexy and lovable?

She half smiled at me. "I'm not going to just go out with anybody, it has to be right. I don't see the point in messing around and getting hurt."

I narrowed my eyes, trying to work out if she was openly judging me. Her eyes were fixed on the road, her face neutral. I opened my mirror and reapplied my lipstick. "I think your standards are too high. You'll never get a boyfriend at this rate. I mean you've never gone for anybody."

She shrugged. "I think he'll come. Otherwise I'll just have to be content with myself. It says in the Bible..."

"Sarah, I don't want to know," I snapped. Just because she believed in all those old fashioned morals, didn't mean she had to inflict them on me. Couldn't she see how irrelevant they were for my life? They worked for her, and I was glad that she was happy, but *I* was happy as I was. I wondered if she would become more liberal at Uni. I mean basically nobody really believed that stuff anymore. Maybe she'd see how ridiculous she was being, she was intelligent enough!

Sarah fell quiet, but I had too much to look forward to, to worry if I'd upset her. She'd get over it. I watched the street lights whiz by with mounting excitement. She pulled the car over to the side of the road and I opened the door. Music was already pumping out from Jen's house, which was where we always had pre-drinks since it was within walking distance of the clubs and bars.

"See you later, lovely," I said, leaning over to kiss my friend on the cheek.

She caught my arm. "Izzy, be sensible," she said seriously. "Please don't do anything stupid."

I freed myself in annoyance. "I'm not a child, Saz, and you're worse than my mother. I'm just going to have fun. The whole point is *not* being sensible. Feeling free." I squeezed her hand. "See you on Monday. I'll ring you tomorrow with the gossip."

I hurried up the cold path as fast as I could without breaking an ankle and rang the doorbell. I waved as Sarah's car melted into the darkness. Jen answered with a squeal, throwing her hands out wide, a bottle of WKD narrowly missing the doorframe.

"Hello, sexy lady!" she cried, giving me a hug. She looked fantastic in a tiny black dress. Her stomach was so flat, the rest of her so curvy I felt a twinge of envy. She ushered me into the kitchen which was littered with glasses, wine and cheap spirits. A black cat watched us lazily from the counter. "Beth's here already. Sue and Tania are coming in half an hour and then we'll make our way over. The boys *should* be there already, but you know what they're like."

She scraped back a kitchen chair over the tiles and pushed the Coke and vodka towards me. Beth appeared from the bathroom and greeted me before going to stroke the cat. "Guess what?" said Jen, leaning forward in excitement. "Will and I got off together last night after school!"

"No!" I exclaimed. "I should get detention more often."

"How far did you two go?" asked Beth.

"Not as far as I plan to go tonight…" she squealed.

We discussed the merits of the boys until Sue and Tania arrived. Sue was wearing so much make-up she looked like a prostitute, not a real person, though I supposed it always got her attention. Tania was overweight but always compensated by showing enormous amounts of chest. They were so close to popping out of the dress completely it was mesmerising. Both girls were already pretty tipsy and I hoped somebody had driven them.

I'd drunk enough to make the walk to the club an easy one. I'd forgotten that it was cold and that my feet hurt. Jen was making a lot of noise and calling to boys across the street. We all laughed at her and the reaction of her victims. I felt light-hearted and brimming with excitement. Away from Sarah I no longer felt like I had to be defensive.

It wasn't late enough for there to be a massive queue outside the club. Only Sue and I were 18, but luckily the bouncers accepted fake IDs; even Jen's, which was in Chinese. The music throbbed and pulsed, echoing inside my chest. The atmosphere drew me down the corridor and onto the smoky dance floor as if in a trance. Everyone looked happy and excited. The lights flashed hypnotically and we started to dance. A group of guys glanced over to us and I felt a few look me up and down. I grinned at the compliment, feeling sexy and alive. How could Sarah not enjoy this? How could she be so dreary and boring? I just needed to get her drunk one night and give her a really good time. It would do her some good to let her hair down.

The music thumped inside me and I swayed, feeling my curves and drinking from a bottle Beth had put into my hand. I started to feel lighter as everything started to blur together. A man put his hands around my waist, his breath stinking of alcohol and smoke, and I shoved him off firmly. Beth gave him eyes and he went to dance with her instead. Jen nudged me in the ribs and gestured to the door.

Tom swaggered in wearing a fashionable shirt and jeans, he was laughing. Luke and Will were at his side, perusing the crowd until they saw us, waved, and then went to get drinks. All three were in the top rugby team for the school and stood a clear head above the rest. Ben followed behind them, forever the unnoticed tag-along. I tousled my hair and shortened my skirt in anticipation.

The boys joined us and at first we danced awkwardly, half a circle to each gender, before Jen grabbed Will to dance with her and I was suddenly facing Tom. He looked at me and I blushed. My heart was racing with excitement and my stomach clenched at his closeness. Did he realise the effect he had on me? What effect did I have on him? The music pounded in my ears, echoing my pulse, coupling with the alcohol to make everything feel like a dream. People barged past as the club became more crowded and I used it as an excuse to get closer to him. His arms slipped around my waist and pushed me into him. His chest was hard and I could feel the lines of his muscles through the thinness of his shirt as I ran my hands up his body to his broad shoulders. He was so almost mine. I felt a shiver of pleasure as his hands took in the curve of my hips and thighs. He found me attractive. I was attractive.

Suddenly his lips found mine, gentle, and then crushing mine with passion. My body exploded in heat, excitement and joy. I was briefly aware of the flash of a camera. I pushed myself closer into his arms, wanting to feel completely accepted by him. Our lips parted, his hands wandered across my whole body. I felt like I could hardly breathe.

I wasn't sure how long we stayed dancing, kissing and drinking, I was too far gone to judge time. I was just perfectly happy. Suddenly something inside him snapped and he grabbed my hand. I looked around me in confusion and vaguely noticed Will and Jen were missing. Tom pulled me through the crowd and suddenly we were out onto the cold street. I blinked and stared around. Were we leaving, or did he just want a smoke? Tom's lips were suddenly crushing mine again and I melted into his arms. He guided me into a taxi, his arm around my waist.

I barely thought to ask where we were going as Tom continued to kiss me on the mouth, jaw, neck. It just felt like bliss. His hand was running up my leg, pushing my skirt above my hips. Suddenly embarrassed in front of the taxi driver, I hurriedly pulled it down again and diverted his hand. He wanted to have sex. The thought thrilled me yet terrified me at the same time. I'd messed around with boys before, but never actually gone all the way. Did I want this? It was Tom! If I didn't do it with him, the most attractive man I'd ever met, who would I do it with? If I didn't do it, I guessed he would be unlikely to take an interest in me again. Fear started to squeeze my stomach and I tried to ignore it. One step at a time. I was in control here. I'd seduced him.

The taxi stopped and Tom pulled me out. We were on a street of cute terraced houses. He led me up a path and fumbled, drunkenly for the key. Once inside he closed the door with his foot and pushed me against the wall, his mouth once again on mine. I could barely breathe. He was just so gorgeous. His hand once again started to pull up my skirt. All of a sudden all my emotions changed. My body stiffened. I didn't want him on me anymore, he was too much, his kisses too wet. His breath stank of cheap beer and vodka, his strength was suddenly intimidating. I wanted to feel loved but all of a sudden I just felt used, a cheap pleasure. I wanted reassurance that what was happening was right. I pushed him away.

Tom looked down at me in puzzlement and ran a hand through his short curly hair. "What's wrong?"

I took a step sideways along the wall to catch my breath.

"I'm sorry; it's just a bit quick. I... can we talk a bit? I mean, I barely know you."

Tom sighed and put both hands behind his head, pacing in frustration. "Izzy, it's two o'clock in the morning and we're both drunk. I want sex, you want sex, it's simple."

His tone was making me feel very cold. Being drunk suddenly made me feel emotional instead of happy. "I'm not sure I want sex now," I said quietly, looking at the floor.

Tom swore in anger. "Then why on Earth did you come displaying all, taunting me with it, kissing me, encouraging me, coming home? You can't treat a man like that. Do you have any idea how I feel right now?"

I was crying now, I couldn't help it. "And you can't treat a woman like this! I'm not just an object for sex."

His voice was thick with rage and drink. "Well you can hardly talk in a club can you? Why else do you walk around in little more than underwear but to be sexually attractive? You want me, I can tell you do. Or are you just frigid?"

I was losing control to tears now. I could barely calm myself to speak. What had gone wrong? I didn't understand.

Tom looked down at me in disgust. I imagined how unattractive I must look with mascara smeared across my face. "Get out of my house, bitch! And next time don't promise what you can't deliver. You came all the way back to my house? To leave me like this?" He hit the wall with his fist.

I kicked off my shoes and ran out of the door. On the street everything started to spin and I grabbed the garden wall to steady myself. Trembling I got my mobile out of my clutch and dialled Sarah's number. It took her a while to pick up and when she did she sounded groggy with sleep.

It took Sarah a while to calm me down to understand enough of what I was saying. "Just come and get me, Saz.

Please come and get me. Please..." I sobbed. I looked around for a street name and hobbled to the end of the road. "Bushdel Road. I'm at the end of Bushdel Road." I collapsed at the foot of the sign and cried into my lap. I just wanted to be home and safe with my flowery duvet and the photos of my friends smiling down from the wall.

I must have dozed off as the next thing I knew Sarah was pulling me up from the floor, wearing a hoody over her pyjamas tucked into bright pink wellies. Her hair was a mess and her eyes puffy from sleep, but she smiled gently down at me and helped me into the car.

She drove in silence back to my house while I took the time to gather myself and we crept into the kitchen. Sarah put on the kettle and started to make some hot chocolate. I sat down and massaged my feet. I hadn't realised before but my toes were bleeding and I had a big blister on each sole. Sarah put a glass of water before me while the kettle boiled.

"Drink so you feel less hungover tomorrow," she ordered.

I obeyed, though I was feeling less drunk already. I could slowly feel myself relax. I wanted my bed. But I also wanted Sarah. Nobody made me feel as safe as her. She stood up to pour the boiling water. "Do you want to talk about it?"

I brought my knees up under my chin. "Not really. Tom said some horrible things to me when I said I wouldn't sleep with him."

Sarah's eyes filled with compassion. "Oh, Izzy. Well at least you didn't sleep with him and find out he was horrible after."

My eyes were filling with tears again. "Oh, Saz, I don't understand what happened. What really went wrong? I *want* to sleep with Tom. It just all got too much."

Sarah's eyes were filling with tears now as well. "Izzy, you don't need to sleep with him. Your value is not in how

20

attractive you are to men. You don't need to lower yourself to trying to attract every man that comes along with your body."

I glared at her. "Of course my value isn't in men!" I snapped. "I just want to have a good time. I want to experience it all. Just because you don't approve of how I dress doesn't mean I'm lowering myself. It's hardly like I stuck out!"

Sarah was crying now as she looked at me. She looked pitying and angry all at the same time and it made me cross, as if she thought she was better than me. "Izzy, it's not meant to be like this. Love, relationships, sex, they're all so good and so special. I hate watching you get hurt again and again. They'll only hurt you more once you start sleeping with these men. Don't you want them to care more about you than your body?"

"You can have both, Sarah. Right now I want to have fun, explore. I had a good time tonight. Do you know how it feels to be singled out and kissed? I can settle down later and fall in love then. Right now the world is so open and free and exciting."

She held my hand gently. "They'll rip your heart and your trust to shreds. Don't you want to put everything you have into that one relationship, make it as special and firm as can be?"

I freed my hand from her grasp. "And so a Christian never got their heart broken, right? Stop judging me. You think you're so pure and wise? I wouldn't live your life for anything!"

For the first time in my life I saw Sarah lose her temper. She pushed back the chair with a squeal. "Fine, Izzy! Go around showing the men what's on offer and enjoy it. I hope it makes you very happy. I'm trying to help and you just throw it all constantly back into my face. Being a Christian is part of who I am, Izzy, you can't just have a go at me every time I mention it." She stormed out of the house and I watched her back in shock. I'd never expected her to snap. I supposed she was tired and so was I. And I was so fed up of her judging me as if my morals were not the norm of our day. I'd never done anything really bad in my life yet Sarah always disapproved of something or other. How could she live a life so constricted by rules and regulations? It would drive me mad. And anyway sex was sex. Sarah was wrong. You could just have good sex with people without being attached to them. And I was hardly promiscuous. Hell, I was still a virgin!

I drained the rest of the hot chocolate and staggered up to bed. I'd make it up to her on the phone tomorrow. To be honest, knowing Sarah, she would probably ring with an apology first. I stripped off my clothes and used a flannel to remove the worst of the make-up before collapsing in bed. Sleep came swiftly.

The next day I didn't wake up until Mum knocked on my door with a thirty-minute warning for lunch. I felt sick and my head was pounding. I certainly didn't feel like a roast lunch. I stumbled into the shower, drank a glass of water and then tried to seem bright for my family. Thankfully, the more food I forced down, the less queasy I became and I managed to eat enough to not hurt Mum's feelings. Kieran and Jack always had seconds anyway. I was glad when nobody asked me how last night had been. I was trying hard not to think about either Tom or Sarah. I wasn't sure how to process it all, what to learn from it.

After the washing up I glanced at my phone. Still no text from Sarah. Well she would have only been home from church a few hours. Maybe I should be the first to apologise. She had, after all, come out to get me in the middle of the night. As I thought about it, I had probably been way too intense about her not coming clubbing as well. I sighed and texted that I hoped she wasn't too tired and that I was sorry for getting her out of bed. I said I was grateful for everything she had done. I didn't apologise for our argument as I didn't feel ready for that yet. I still felt a little angry at her.

I spent the rest of the afternoon reading and watching iPlayer, nursing my hangover. Still no reply from Sarah. I tried their home number but no response. They must be out on one of their family walks or church lunches or something. I had a text conversation with Jen about what she'd got up to last night but her exaggerations and forced mysteries felt repetitive and dull. By nine o'clock I was feeling suitably bored, ill and tried to go to bed. I put my phone on loud so I could read Sarah's text as soon as it came through. Had I managed to damage my most important friendship?

Kieran woke me up and my head was pounding again. It was very dark, why on Earth was he in here? I glanced at my clock and groaned. 6:30 am! I mumbled for him to leave.

"Get up and get a dressing gown, Isabelle. There are some policemen wanting to speak with you at the door."

I frowned and sat up, pausing while the room span. My stomach squirmed. Policemen? Had not all our party got home the night before last? Had somebody trashed something? Had Jen done something stupid?

I grabbed hold of my dressing gown and followed Kieran down the stairs. My feet still hurt with every step. Kieran led me to the door and then held me by the shoulders. I wondered why, he was never normally affectionate. I'd never accepted him as my new dad.

"Miss Maids?" asked one of the policemen. I nodded. "Do you know what Sarah Holland was doing yesterday late afternoon? Had you two been in contact?"

My body went cold, and I put one hand against the wall. "No. I last saw her in the middle of Saturday night. She didn't reply to my text yesterday. What happened?"

"You weren't planning on meeting up?"

"No, tell me what happened?" I demanded more urgently.

The two policemen glanced at each other and gave me sympathetic looks. "We regret to inform you that Sarah Holland was hit by a driver we believe to have been drunk, at the junction at the end of the road yesterday evening at 6pm. She was taken to hospital but passed away an hour later. Her injuries were severe. We're so sorry. We are trying to work out what she was doing after church. Her parents believed she may have been coming over to visit you."

I stared at them in shock. This couldn't be true, it was impossible. Then Kieran was walking me back into the house and sitting me down. I couldn't take in my surroundings, couldn't take in Mum's hug. Sarah was dead. She was dead. And the last words I had said to her were in anger.

"Though the earth give way and the mountains fall into the heart of the sea."

Chapter Two

Life seemed to lose meaning after Sarah died. Everything seemed pointless. What was the point of school, work, conversation, reading when you could just die at such a young age and everything you worked for was for nothing? It felt so wrong, so very, very wrong. People like Sarah, healthy, intelligent, kind, shouldn't die at the age of seventeen. It almost felt like if I didn't accept it, it wouldn't be true and that she would come back.

I was in a permanent daze in the three days up to the funeral. I couldn't eat, sleep or talk. Nothing seemed worthwhile anymore. I just couldn't care about anything when everything was so unimportant compared to death. It was almost a shock to find myself suddenly in a church next to Mum, with a scattering of school friends and teachers around me, most of the faces strangers.

I hadn't been in a church since the junior school concerts we used to do. Grandad's funeral had been in a side chapel at a crematorium, but not a big old building like this with banners on the walls and modern seats that were packed with people. It seemed right that Sarah's story ended here, in the place that meant so much to her. That one coherent thought was enough to bring tears to my eyes and I bit my tongue to distract myself.

The funeral was a bit of a blur. The songs were surprisingly upbeat for a funeral, all focused on praising God, and we were informed they were Sarah's favourites. I tried to sing them for Sarah's sake, but my voice kept catching and I struggled to read the words through tears. The Bible readings were all about God's goodness and Heaven and some things that I didn't really understand, but sounded wise and old. Looking at the vicar's smiling face and the smiles of some of those in the congregation I became jealous of their confidence that Sarah was happy and in Heaven. Didn't they realise that she was gone? Cold and mashed up and about to be covered in soil? But I suppose that was the whole point of religion, right? An emotional crutch to take away the ugliness of the world and fill it with beauty and hope, so that the unbearable became bearable. For a second I longed for the same feeling of reassurance that Sarah had gone to this amazing place, but then it just felt childish and deceiving. Sarah was dead and I was never going to see her again. There was no point in convincing yourself of a lie. Yet, still I was strangely comforted by the vicar's words. There had to be some good in this situation. Something purposeful and full of hope, or it became too horrible to bear.

Sarah's father came up next to speak through tears and laughter. He talked about his beloved, beautiful, generous, servant hearted daughter and the memories of her childhood. I was crying so much it was hard to stay silent. Mum squeezed my hand gently. Then he talked about her death.

"Sarah was barely conscious when she was brought to the hospital but, thanks to the goodness of God, Merylin and I made it in time before she slipped away. She knew that she

26

was probably going to die and she wanted us to tell everyone... not to be upset but," he paused to catch his voice through the tears, "...but to be happy, so happy because she was going to Heaven. She'd run the race and made it! She said she was excited because she was leaving the sufferings and struggles of the world behind to be with Jesus..." He paused again and quiet weeping echoed around the church. "She was happy and wants us to be happy too, however much we miss her... She also wanted us to show our forgiveness to Paul Merl, the driver who crashed into her. She didn't want anyone to harbour bad feelings against him. Merylin and I wish to publicly declare our acceptance of that now. That we forgive Paul and... and we wish him well." Such a Sarah thing to say. How was I ever meant to forgive the man careless enough to get drunk and take her from the world without reason? He deserved every punishment he could receive for killing her. "And finally she asked that her non-Christian friends explore the thing that brought her the most happiness and joy in her life, her faith, and that she longed to be able to see them again someday in Heaven." Sarah's dad folded the paper and sat back down next to his wife, comforting her with an arm. Sarah's last words made me feel uncomfortable. Surely Christianity was only something you believed if you wanted to, if you wanted to embrace a different way of life and culture. It would only work for some people, normally those who'd got used to it as children. What exactly did Sarah mean by 'explore' it? Go to a church service? Ask somebody? Follow some of the rules?

After a final hymn that many people belted out, we were all welcomed to stay for a bring-and-share lunch. People started to make huddles and chattered together. Some even laughed. Here and there weeping people were being comforted. I just felt alone. How could people act normally when Sarah had just died? And in such a strange place full of strange words.

Jen came over to sit next to me while our mums chatted. When it was clear I wasn't in the mood for talking, she turned all her attention to Leonie behind us. I just wanted Sarah. She would have been the only one who could have comforted me now, and she was the only one I couldn't have.

People were gathering around Jen and my mum, so I slipped away to get a drink and some quiet.

"Izzy?" came a quiet voice.

I turned to see Sarah's mum coming towards me. Her eyes were red and swollen, but she was smiling. She held out her hands to me and then embraced me. "Izzy, I wanted to thank you for all the close years of friendship you showed my daughter. I know how much you loved each other." Her words hit me too hard for me to speak. "Before she died, she asked me to give you her Bible. It was very dear to her." She fished out a zip-up book cover bag with the Christian fish sewn onto it. "Treasure it well, and know you are welcome at any time around our house still, we would love to see you."

"Thank you," I managed around the lump in my throat. "I was so lucky to have been her friend. The night before she died... she picked me up because I was too drunk to get home... She was so kind. Our last conversation was an argument. And then if she hadn't been coming to visit me... I'm so sorry…"

"Stop, Izzy," said Merylin firmly. "Of course it wasn't your fault, any more than it was for me to have bought her the car, or for us deciding to move here. This wasn't something decided by man. God called her to be with Him in Heaven. She's safe now, we think of Heaven as 'home'."

I shook my head. "I don't want her to go to Heaven," I

wept. "I want her here. I need her. God didn't need to take her so young! Why couldn't he wait? It's just so unfair!"

"She'd fulfilled her purpose on Earth. It was God's plan for her. And now she's happy with Him," said her mother in the gentle way Sarah had often used to speak about her faith. When I had let her.

I squeezed her shoulder. "I'll never forget her."

She smiled. "Come around any time you want, Izzy, we mean that."

When she walked off I felt so alone again. I grabbed Mum and asked if we could leave.

Back home on my bed I traced the fish sewn onto the cover bag. Why had Sarah given me her Bible? Why not give it to one of her Christian friends who could appreciate it? It meant nothing to me. Other than it was hers, anyway.

I unzipped it and opened it before me. On one side a soft, leather bound Bible was strapped into place with Velcro. On the other side was a deep pocket full of folded bits of paper and a pink notebook. I opened some of the bits of paper curiously. They were notes on Bible passages and sermons, and random church handouts or newsletters. I put them back carefully and then freed the notebook. I flicked through its pages. It was a diary. Immediately I felt guilty and shut it again. Sarah had given me her Bible, surely she hadn't meant for me to have her private diary as well? It could say all sorts of things she never wanted anyone to know. I debated whether to send it back to her parents. That would probably be the most honest thing to do. I ran my hand up and down the smooth cover. Then again it had been put with her Bible and her mother had given it to me... I suddenly realised I really, really wanted it, because while I had it, it was like having Sarah back. Reading all her thoughts and feelings would be like talking to her again. While

I had it, I would still have her. Her thoughts, feelings and opinions could live on.

I took the notebook and slipped it under my pillow. I turned back and opened the Bible. In the front cover were words written by Sarah's parents. '*To our darling daughter, on her baptism. We will always be so proud of you. We pray that you'll grow up into a spiritually mature woman, with Christ at the centre of your life, always.*' Well Sarah hadn't grown up at all! I thumped the Bible closed again while tears started to pour down my cheeks. It just wasn't fair. How could Sarah die? If there really was a God, there would be justice in the world and Sarah would have never died. There wouldn't be death at all!

"When what is vile is honoured by men."

Chapter Three

It was our last ever lesson at school. I liked the philosophy element of religious studies because the teacher was so relaxed. Most of my school year were worrying about exams, but I had barely given them any thought. Sarah had worked hard and it hadn't got her anywhere. The teacher had written potential essay questions on the board. I felt like we'd done the subjects to death over the last two years.

"Jen, what would you write about in this one?" asked Miss Berry. "*'The pros and cons of Anselm's ontological argument according to Thomas Aquinas and Descartes?'*"

"That it's ridiculous and makes no sense?" replied Jen. Giggles surrounded her.

Miss Berry was completely unfazed. "Good, you've got yourself a conclusion. Now convince me with your paragraph headings."

I switched off and wondered what Sarah would have made of all this. She'd never used any fancy old arguments or plays on words to defend God. I imagined her meeting Thomas Aquinas with his monk robe and bald head up in Heaven and smiled. Would they argue about what God was like? Would they agree? In religious studies she had often been vocal but pushing the conversation down a different avenue to what the teacher intended.

"Izzy," announced the teacher making me jump. "This one. 'In your opinion what argument is the most convincing for the existence of God: the ontological argument, cosmological argument, miracles or personal experience?'"

I sighed. "Personal experience," I mumbled. She had told us that over and over.

"Good. Why?"

"All the rest are subject to opinion, but nobody can dispute what you yourself have experienced," I replied. Miss Berry nodded and turned back to the board. "Miss Berry, I don't think Sarah would have said that."

The teacher froze, clearly unsure how to handle the sensitive topic. "What do you think Sarah would have argued?" she asked at last, gently.

I shrugged, twiddling my blonde hair around my fingers. "I'm not sure. But she was convinced of God's existence and never once said 'because I can feel him' or 'I once heard his voice' or whatever. Surely our experience is subjective too? Many people can see the same thing but interpret it in different ways. Surely if people from mutually exclusive religions all have personal experiences some of them must be wrong, in their heads, I mean?"

Miss Berry nodded. "And that is a good point to put in your essay, though remember you'll have to combat that with another pro if you're going to maintain your conclusion in the exam." She turned back to the board and I felt frustrated. Couldn't she see this wasn't just about the exam?

"Miss Berry," I asked. "What do you believe?"

She smiled at me. "I believe there is a God and that we can access him in many different ways. We can all sense something

32

beyond the norm and all ways to access that are equal as long as they don't harm others."

"So you're a pluralist? But then why do religions say the others are wrong?" I asked.

"Because each in itself is true and is the *one* truth, but all truths are equal overall."

I raised an eyebrow. "That makes no sense. Two contradictions can't both be true."

Miss Berry smiled. "Ah, we have somebody who thinks like a scientist in the room. George! 'Are science and God mutually exclusive?'"

I sighed, frustrated. Maybe religion was just whatever you wanted it to be to make you happy, even if it didn't make sense. Sarah had always seemed to ignore those parts of Christianity that didn't make sense. A man 2000 years ago rising from the dead? A flood that covered the world? Creation in seven days? Maybe they were just tools to access something deeper, something that couldn't be put into words. In Miss Berry's language, truths to access the underlying truth, even if they weren't by themselves true. So the Bible could be treated like stories with underlying truths. Sarah hadn't believed that. She'd quoted one of the writers once, saying something like, if Jesus hadn't really risen from the dead, it would be better for Christians to be dead, or something. Why was the whole topic so confusing? So many strongly held opinions. It was just so much easier not to think about it.

*

In the end I realised the only way to get people to leave me alone was to revise all the time. That stopped Mum's criticism of how I needed to 'move on' and Kieran's awkward looks. It

33

gave me an excuse to not go out and see my friends. I just wanted to be on my own. So I worked, imagining Sarah revising in her own house. She had wanted to be a doctor and had always worked so hard... The image of her studying spurred me on. Maybe I could work for the both of us.

The two weeks of study leave flew by quickly, and then came exams. English, history, religious studies. I felt myself cross them off one by one as I did the modules and then forgot them. As we filed out of the last exam I felt better than I had since before Sarah had died. It was over. School was finished. Forever. I took a moment to work out all the strange emotions inside me. I was so relieved I'd got through the exams without being ill for one or forgetting to revise something. I was so excited to be going to Uni. Yet I was also terrified of all the changes. And I was going to miss my school friends, especially Sarah.

"Hey, Izzy!" cried Jen, flinging her arms around me. "We're freeeeeeeee!" she squealed. "We're going down to the river, wanna come?"

I smiled and gave in. "Love to."

"Brill, you get crisps and snacks on your way. Sue's gone to get drinks, and Tania's getting the plates and bowls blah blah." Suddenly she drew in closer. "Guess what? I'm not sure you're meant to know but Beth's got a boyfriend. I'm trying to get her to bring him, but apparently he's *working*." She rolled her eyes. "Right, see you there in twenty."

She leapt away and ran to Will, slipping herself under his arm from behind. I still wasn't sure if they were an official couple or not. She certainly liked to parade around with him. She was always so confident. Suddenly, out of nowhere, I realised I disliked her. It shocked me. She was one of my closest friends, wasn't she? But she was vain and crude and

34

selfish and sometimes, just plain nasty. I shook my head. Where had that all come from? I always had such a laugh with Jen. It had to be because I was missing Sarah. I missed her so much.

I hurried home and got changed. This afternoon I was going to forget that Sarah had died. She'd wanted us to be happy so I would. I'd had enough of over thinking everything. Who cared if there was a God or not? I didn't need him anyway. I'd finished exams. I was eighteen, single and free. Life was good.

I flung on a yellow summer dress over my bikini and rooted in the wardrobe for where my flip-flops were buried. Then I more carefully did my make-up. I wanted to feel sexy and in control again.

I bumped into Sue and Tania in Tesco's. Sue had obviously spent a long time on her make-up and straightening her hair this morning even before an exam! I had no idea how she managed to do that! She was carrying a basket full of beer and bottles of cider. We laughed and joked in the queue, ignoring the looks from the old people who dominated the shop at midday. Tania's breath stank of smoke. She'd recently taken up smoking, not only in a casual context but several times a day, to try to lose weight.

We linked arms as we sauntered down to the wide flood plains. Sue swung her bag, making the bottles and cans clink and rattle. A car drove past blasting out loud music and Jen hung out the window to shout at us. Behind her boys wolf whistled.

We laughed and whistled back and then hurried to where it screeched to a halt at the edge of the town where the fields began. Beth and Claire were sitting on the stile waiting for us. Beth looked like she'd been crying and Claire held her hand. I left Sue and Tania with Jen and the boys and hurried over to her.

"What's wrong, hun?" I asked, pulling myself up onto the fence beside her.

She sniffed and stayed looking straight ahead. "Biology went really badly this morning. I think I failed. How am I going to get into Nottingham now?"

"Oh, Beth," I said, giving her a sideward squeeze. "You'll be happy wherever you get in. Everyone loves Uni. It doesn't really matter where you go."

"Yes it does, Izzy! I loved Nottingham and I loved their course. I don't want to end up in London, I'll hate it there. Too many people and the tube and everything."

Claire leant in. "Let's not worry about this now, Beth. Now's the time to celebrate leaving school."

"That's right, baby," shouted Jen as she caught the end of the conversation. "It's time to par-tay! Who's up for a swim?"

She tore across the field, flinging off her dress as she ran and showing her underwear. We followed, though it was hard to run in flip-flops. Soon we were all splashing each other in the river. The boys, of course, had to be more hardcore and all jumped from the bridge into the deeper water. They then proceeded to try to beat each other with more and more crazy summersaults. I scanned them all quickly again to make sure Tom wasn't there. I didn't think I could look him in the eye after what had happened.

We contented ourselves with paddling, our feet sinking into the thick, warm mud. I watched the little silver fish dart between us with sudden flashes of light. I waded in slightly deeper until the current and tangled weeds started to tug at my legs. Sarah had always loved paddling in the river and trying to catch the little fish in plastic bags.

The boys swam and staggered up to us, their hair dripping into their eyes. Will grabbed Jen from behind who squealed and laughed as he flung her into the deeper water. Jonny swung an arm around my shoulder and with the other grabbed Sue, pulling us into him on either side. Skin brushed skin as his hip snuggled into my waist, sending a strange feeling through my stomach.

"Ladies," he announced loudly. "You both look sorely in need of a drink." He marched us out of the water and we flopped down onto towels as he tipped the bags of beer upside down and tossed us a can each. Sue squealed as she opened hers and the contents fizzed everywhere. I laughed, hard, as her leg was covered in a sticky mess and she went back into the water to wash it off. People were calling for beers now and John threw them out, not caring if they hit people or the water. James mock dived for one, splashing Tania who screamed. Drops of water sparkled like diamonds in the sunlight.

I opened my beer carefully and took a cool sip. The sun was hot on my face and I felt a ripple of relaxation spread through me. Exams were over. It was all really over. Now was the time I could let go. I wanted to feel free. I drank deeply, the bubbles tickling my throat.

Mark flopped down beside me. Jonny was now wrestling with Will in the water and the girls all hurried out to avoid the splashing and settled down to sunbathe. I could see Mark was looking me up and down with his dark eyes and pretended not to notice.

"You doing anything this summer, Izzy?" he asked, slightly awkwardly.

"I'm going to France with the family, you?" I took another sip of the beer.

He shrugged. "Will, Jonny, Tom and I are off to Scotland for a bit. Then there's Glastonbury. Not really sure what I'm going to do with myself the rest of the time."

Jen noisily struggled out of the water and dived down between us. "What you two nattering about?" she asked with a grin. "Have you heard the news? Hannah Stanly's had a baby! She's what, sixteen? I wonder if she'll give it up for adoption. Apparently she's staying in school."

"No!" said Mark. "I'd thought she was just fat! Who's the dad?"

Jen shrugged. "No idea. Don't know who'd want to sleep with *her* anyway."

I frowned. "Don't be mean, Jen! Poor girl must be terrified. Maybe she just wanted somebody to love."

Jen frowned at me, unused to being challenged, then shrugged. "Anyone stupid enough to not use protection or the morning after pill is too stupid to look after a baby while in school. She's screwed up her whole life."

Jen's words hit me deeply for some unknown reason. I'd never really cared about what flowed out of her mouth before, but now it made me angry. "Don't be so nasty! Maybe all she wants is to be a mum."

"Oh, so being a teenage mum is a good idea then?" she bit back, a gleam entering into her eyes.

"Of course not, but..." I started.

"Is that why you went all frigid with Tom? Are you *scared*? There are other forms of protection other than being a virgin, you know." She laughed and I blushed. She was so nasty and I just hadn't seen it before. I'd just thought we were all normal. Everyone discusses people behind their backs, makes jokes at their expense, except Sarah... Sarah... I felt tears warming my eyes.

Jen smirked and turned to go back into the water. I stood. I wanted to leave. I just wanted to be with Sarah. Saz had always been my safe place, the one I could tell anything to.

Mark grabbed my arm. "Don't go, Izzy. Stay. Everyone knows Jen is a bitch. Ignore her. Come on, have another beer."

I smiled down at him, grateful for his support. Mark liked me I realised. He was nice if not as good looking as Tom. I considered sitting back down, laughing at Jen with him to make me feel better. Having more beer until I was drunk and without worries and concerns. He'd get bolder, maybe kiss me, stroke my stomach. That would be nice to feel sexy again, but... That's not what I wanted. How did I know Mark was different from Tom? I'd not spoken to him much outside of a group context. Was it all about sex for him too? Was that the only reason he was being nice? I just wanted Sarah, and there was only one way I felt I could be with her again.

I smiled apologetically down at Mark. "You guys have fun without me." I pulled on my dress, the fabric immediately clinging to the wet bikini, and headed back across the long grass. I watched the grass seeds sticking to my wet feet. Out of the corner of my eye Mark looked as if he might follow, but then Will called him into the river.

I tried to get a grip of myself as I walked home. Why had I got so angry? What was wrong with me? I was meant to feel happy now exams were over. I passed three people in the year below in hoodies despite the sun. They were smoking something sweet beneath the bushes. I'd always discounted them before as the 'bad' people. The ones who didn't care about school, and missed class and stole things. They were the ones who wouldn't go anywhere in the world, except jail anyway. But why did I think that? What made them bad and Jen good? Just because she attended school and was on track for a good Uni? She'd probably tried drugs, but was it drugs that made you a good or bad person? Was it your attitude to life? Your upbringing? Maybe those three had had parents on drugs. Did that excuse them, make them less bad? Was anyone truly bad? Yes, of course some people were truly bad like Hitler and Stalin and mass murderers and rapists. So where was the line? Did you have to be a murderer to be a bad person? Did I have any right to call Jen nasty? Everyone seemed to be a mixture of good and bad. Maybe the question was, is anyone truly good?

I kicked a stone. What was wrong with my head? I had never used to think about philosophy while walking down the street. What was the point of thinking about things which had no answer? Maybe I should have stayed with Mark and just tried to be normal for an afternoon.

I slipped the key into our front door and let myself in. Jack was already home from school and I could hear the sound of him shooting on his Xbox. I showered away the river water from my skin and changed into my comfy pyjamas. I stretched across my bed listening to the birds through my open window and closed my eyes. I imagined Sarah sat at the bottom of the bed reading or choosing us a film.

"God," I whispered into my bedroom. "If you're real, why did you take her? If you're real, why are there children down the road on drugs? Why is Hannah pregnant all alone? Why are boys drawn to girls sexually more than emotionally? You've decided to make a pretty messed up world."

I smiled at myself. Of course God didn't exist. He would make it obvious if he did, not hide behind confusing, subjective philosophy! If he existed there would be justice. We would be born equal, so we could decide for ourselves whether we would be good or bad, not born to drug users or abandoned by our parents or born rich or poor. How had Sarah believed with such certainty? Had she just not been able to cope with a messed up world?

I reached under my bed and brought out the zip up jacket with her Bible and diary. I looked at the Bible for a moment, stroking the soft leather. How was it meant to work? Were you meant to just read it and magically meet God? Was it that its wisdom was unearthly or something? I slipped it out of its pocket and opened it carefully trying to not let any of the slips of paper that Sarah had left, fall out. I knew that it was in two halves, the Old Testament and the New. The Old was really old and the New had Jesus in it. I flicked to where the New began and hesitantly started to read. The first book was called Matthew. I assumed he was the author.

'The book of the genealogy of Jesus Christ, the son of David, the son of Abraham. Abraham was the father of Isaac...'

I scanned down. So many long ridiculous names and they went on for ages! How had Sarah read this? And it already didn't make sense! How could there be two generations between Abraham and Jesus as well as... I quickly scanned all the names to the end... three lots of fourteen... forty-two? And why did it matter?

I closed the Bible. Maybe Sarah would have been able to explain it to me. Or maybe it was the sort of thing that was meant to be mysterious and unexplainable? I shook my head. Why wasn't anything straightforward?

I carefully tucked the Bible back and instead took Sarah's diary out. It was a small, pink, ring bound notebook. It looked like a sticker of some sort had once been on the front which Sarah had half removed with her nails.

Reverently I opened it as if it was all that was left of her life. Her neat writing was crammed onto the lines and flowers and fruit were doodled in the corners. I turned to the front page.

'Dear God,

Thank you for such a beautiful sunny day today and thank you that Izzy and I had such a lovely time at the park. I am worried about her though. She kept on talking about Tom and I'm worried she's going to do something stupid. She barely knows him! Please keep her safe and protect her self-esteem. Show her that Your way is the best way. Please give me the words to say. I always feel so clumsy trying to advise her. Please let her know how much You love her. I also pray that Anna will feel better soon with her tummy bug. I also heard that Hannah S is pregnant. Only You know what she must be going through. Please help her, God! Thank you that You're always there for me. I love You. Please keep me faithful.

Amen.'

I tried to bite back tears. Oh, Sarah, I miss you! I remembered that Saturday in the park, must have been about six months ago. We'd sat on the swings for hours and talked. I'd probably gone on and on and on about Tom. How had she put up with me?

The next prayer was about people I didn't know in her church so I skipped it. The next one had tear stains across the ink.

'Dear God,

I met Izzy's mum's new boyfriend today. They don't respect each other at all; they constantly criticise and swear at each other. It makes me so upset that this is Izzy's model for relationships. I think of all the relationships she's had and that she never wants to mention her father. Her mum must be hurting so deeply inside. She reminds me of the woman at the

42

well who You helped when nobody else could. Please help and heal them, God. Please help her mum realise that human relationships will never fully satisfy, only a relationship with You can. That You are there to love her unconditionally. Please help Izzy see that not all men are bad, so that it doesn't affect her trust for people and she doesn't learn to let men use her. Please, please, please let all three of them become Christians. I want that so much!

Amen.'

I sighed. Oh, Sarah, you know nothing, you were always so innocent of the way the world works. People and relationships can't be perfect just by wishing for them. I flicked through the rest of the prayers to see how far they went. About three quarters of the book was full. The last entry was the Sunday she had died. It must have been hours before the accident. I wasn't ready to read that yet.

In the front cover Sarah had written, '*Your cross changes everything.*' What did she mean by that? She sounded fanatical.

I heard Mum shut the front door and stomp up the stairs. She peeked her head around my door. "How's my super clever girl? I hadn't expected to find you here! Why aren't you with your friends, celebrating?"

I shrugged in reply. Mum gave me a knowing glance and flicked her fringe from her eyes. "Come on then. Let's go out for dinner to celebrate. Kieran's working late, but Jack can come too. How's that sound?"

I smiled. "Thanks, Mum. Sounds great."

"But you trusted in your beauty."

Chapter Four

The summer went so quickly even though it was the longest holiday I had ever had. Mum and Kieran split up the day I got my results and found out I'd got into Bristol University to study history. Mum put on a brave face, however, and baked me a cake. I tried to be strong for her and pretend everything was normal, even though I knew she drank the whisky under her bed every evening just so she could sleep. She went out more with her friends and I felt like her mother, worrying when she got back late or not at all.

My heart was pounding as Mum drove me down to Bristol, the car full of boxes of things I wasn't even sure if I would need, but I was glad for a new start. I wanted to be away from the house, and away from people who always thought about Sarah every time they saw me. Maybe I could make better friends here, be more careful who I spent time with. There must be plenty of people who were genuinely kind and caring. No more Jens. I felt heady with excitement and nerves. I desperately wanted to fit in there. I wanted to feel like I truly belonged.

The nearer and nearer we got, the tighter my stomach clenched until I almost felt sick. Would people like me? What if I didn't get on with my flatmates? What if I'd forgotten something crucial for my course?

My first sight of Bristol was the suspension bridge over the River Avon and it caught me off guard. I'd never expected to find a city beautiful, I much preferred open fields, woods and narrow streets with wonky stone cottages, however Bristol just was. The river ran in a sort of ravine with sheer rocky cliffs either side. At the top of one cliff clustered colourful houses as if we were at the seaside. Mum informed me that was the edge of Clifton, where her mum had grown up. She put on a posh accent as she said it and sounded so dreadful I smiled through my nerves. Then we were driving down beside the muddy river with the suspension bridge rearing above us and then over us. A road warning sign flashed past with a crocodile on it and I shook my head with surprise. Had I imagined that? It had to be a joke.

Suddenly we were driving up a ridiculously steep, winding road up the cliff side, trees bending over, fighting for the light above us. Mum mentioned when she was really small her mum had brought her back here to watch peregrine falcons diving off the cliffs over the river. The way she described her old Bristol was almost like a fairy tale. We had to stop halfway up the hill in a traffic jam and I was so glad I wasn't driving with my shocking hill starts. I'd deliberately avoided driving since I'd passed my test and Bristol wasn't looking like the place I would want to restart in.

"Of course Bristol was a dump back then, when I was really small," said Mum, breaking the fairy tale. "But since then they're meant to have replaced the worse areas with big shopping centres." She put a hand on my lap and then had to quickly take it back to release the handbrake as the traffic stop-started. "It has everything for you, my sweet. It's quirky, arty yet lots of science stuff too. All that shopping, theatres, cinemas, clubs, cafes. You have so many places to explore. They even have a hot air balloon festival." She studied my face, her eyes flickering to where my lip had swollen from being chewed all the way here. "There's nothing to worry about, Izzy. These will be the best years of your life."

I suddenly felt the burden to enjoy myself more than ever. There was such a cultural expectation for me to be happy. Even without my family. Without Sarah.

I was glad we didn't have to go all the way into the city to reach Stoke Bishop where my hall was. I liked the feeling of being perched on the edge, like a falcon on those cliffs. I could fly away and escape if I needed. We passed the zoo on the right and I thought how fun it would be to visit with a big group of friends where we could all act like children for the day. There was something very cool about living a few minutes from a zoo. Then there were neat, pretty terraces of old Victorian houses with ridiculously big windows and tiny gardens. The hill behind them fell away at an alarming rate and I realised I was going to get fit walking around here. The empty green space continued on my left. I felt myself relax as I realised I wasn't going to be hemmed in. My mum announced the green space to be 'The Downs' quickly followed by a demand not to ever walk there at night on my own. I mumbled a promise in response and watched the dog walkers as we turned to drive through the park to the far side. Some people were even flying kites. A group of people in sports kits were letting themselves be shouted at aggressively by an angry looking instructor. I would have felt sorry for them if they hadn't been the ones who'd signed up for it. I couldn't help but compare myself to the scantily clad runners who jogged past. I'd barely done any exercise this summer and I regretted it now when I looked at how my stomach sagged when I leant over. I'd need to join a gym or something.

Then the trees became thicker and big houses loomed between them surrounded by private gardens. To me it looked even posher than Clifton. We followed the signs to 'Durdham Hall' and slowly managed to weave around students, piles of boxes and cars at all sort of angles in the car park. An older student in a reflective jacket was desperately trying to get people to park in specific spots or move on. Everywhere students and their parents were wandering around trying to not look lost or heaving bags, snapping at each other. Some parents were even crying. It was so strange not knowing anyone at all. I took a deep breath, clinging to the car door handle, preparing to enter the chaos. Mum was already opening the boot and righting objects that had fallen over. I took another deep breath and whispered under my breath, *'Come on, Izzy, it will be fine. People liked you at school, they'll like you here. It'll be fun, lots of new friends, parties and clubbing and drinking. Absolute freedom. You'll enjoy it; just get out of the car. Stop being an idiot.'*

At a very busy reception where all the students available to help seemed to be Asian, I was told I was in a flat in C Block and gained a key and a code. We trudged back to the car and grabbed as many of the bags and boxes as we could carry before stumbling around the back of the complex of buildings to find my flat. I gave nervous smiles to those students we passed, trying desperately to memorise faces. So many people seemed more confident than me.

The flat was cleaner than I had expected. The walls and doors were all cream with a dark blue carpet. There were marks from previous tenants but nothing drastic. The front door opened onto a corridor with six closed doors, all unmarked except for fire door warning signs. Mum dumped her load outside the front and then went to get a second. The closed doors were intimidating, cold. I paused, suddenly alone, hesitating before knocking on the first to my left.

A short girl with long, dark hair opened it and smiled, nervously. "Chloe," she said, holding out her hand. She held her head tilted back a little further than normal and I wondered if it was the arrogance of somebody used to being in charge, or just because she was short.

"Izzy," I replied slightly awkwardly, dropping a bag so I could shake her hand back. I couldn't remember the last time I had shook somebody's hand. "Do you know which room is mine?"

"The two at the end on the right are still free," she said waving a hand. "That door is the kitchen, that's the bathroom. Let me know when you've finished unpacking and we can have some tea and cake. My granny baked me one."

I smiled. "Sounds nice, thanks." I shuffled down the rest of the corridor, trying to guess what sort of person Chloe was from her appearance and manner, with the strange sensation that I'd know her well by the end of the year.

My bedroom was a lot smaller than I was used to, but I had my own sink and the window was large, looking straight out onto the central courtyard between all the blocks. So many people my age milled around there with parents in tow. I felt very small.

I dumped my bags on the empty mattress and quickly unzipped them. I desperately wanted the items which would make this room a sanctuary, a home. I found the photo frames with my family in from our recent trip to France and put them on my desk. My laptop, my bedding, my books with their creased covers from over reading...

I heard a knock on the front door and hurried to let Mum in with the next load. "I think I just saw your future husband, darling."

I rolled my eyes. "Mum!"

"Nice face, tall, broad shoulders, smiley." She grinned as she dumped a box of rattling saucepans.

"Tell me again in ten years' time. Mum, can you put those in the kitchen?"

She sighed as she bent down to pick them up again. "You can be bossy you know, Izzy."

I held the ridiculously heavy door open for her and she dumped them on our kitchen table. The sides were already covered in bags and boxes from my new flatmates. The place was a tip.

When Mum had ferried the last of the boxes she sat on the bed watching me unpack for half an hour, nibbling on a sandwich. She always seemed to eat with exaggerated delicacy which sometimes seemed an accusation of everyone else's eating habits. Kieran had made it into a running joke that we'd all got tired of. There was nothing else she could do since I wanted to unpack everything in a certain way. Finally she gave me a kiss and left me to it. It was weird that it might be Christmas before I next saw her. I'd never been away from home more than a week before.

After two hours I felt my room was in reasonable order and I shoved the remainder of the unpacking under my bed. My friends all smiled down at me from photos on my walls. '*Look how popular and fun you are*!' they cried. They gave me confidence. My favourite fiction books brought colour and security to my shelves. I touched up my make-up in the mirror so I could make a positive first impression. I needed to put on my best side.

I wandered down the corridor to Chloe's room and knocked hesitantly on the door. I heard a muffled greeting so entered. A blonde girl with glasses sat next to Chloe on the bed and a guy in a grey hoodie lounged on the desk chair that he pushed back and forth in discomfort. They were all eating a glistening chocolate cake that sat on the floor between them.

"Hi," I ventured into the already awkward atmosphere. "I'm Izzy."

"Anna," smiled the blonde girl, waving. She wore a flowery dress and bright pink cardigan. She had a wide mouth with creases that indicated she smiled a lot. It was the sort of mouth that ruled out red lipstick, yet pulled off the natural look beautifully.

"Fred," nodded the boy. I decided he was trying too hard to look cool.

There was a prolonged silence as I perched on the edge of the bed and Chloe handed me a slice of cake in kitchen roll. She mentioned the other two flatmates were Mike and Holly. "Where are you from and what are you studying?" she ventured.

"Cambridgeshire. I'm doing history." I tried to smile confidently and not to let crumbs of cake get stuck in my lip gloss. Why, oh why had I just reapplied it?

"Mike's doing history too," said Anna. "You'll be able to find all your lectures together. Holly and I are medics. Those two are engineers."

"Though I'm a mechanical, and she's a civil," said Fred, in an off-hand voice as if even he was bored by what he was saying.

I nodded as if I understood the difference. There was a pause. "Looks like they did a nice job of matching us," I said just to break the silence.

Everyone nodded in unison. Another awkward silence. "Has everyone seen the Hall meeting at 3pm?" said Anna, unfolding a timetable. "We've got just under an hour. Then there's dinner. Then an evening run by the JCR, whatever that is."

"Junior Common Room," explained Chloe. "They're the second years who stay in Hall."

We all nodded again. I finished my cake and unable to bear the awkwardness any more, decided to start unpacking my kitchen things.

A guy that I assumed was Mike was in the kitchen unloading crates of beer into the fridge. Somebody had propped the heavy kitchen door open with a dictionary even though it said '*Fire door. Keep closed at all times*!' so he didn't notice when I entered. I awkwardly stood behind him for a minute thinking about how to introduce myself.

"Hi," I ventured. "I hear you're studying history too?"

He turned and smiled. I realised as he stood straight that he was very tall. He wore Jack Wills trackies with designer boxers peeping over the top and large fashion glasses. I rebelliously thought he had probably been turned down by Oxbridge and ended up here. "Yeah, you Izzy?"

"Er, yeah. I see you came prepared," I said, nodding to the fridge.

"Yeah, beats cake don't you think. Want one? It will help you meet all these people."

He held out a beer. I actually didn't feel like one at all with all the unpacking, but I couldn't damage an offer of friendship. I took it and thanked him. Then it hit me. We really could live however we wanted here. Nobody would tell us off for drinking in the day; parents didn't know and would even expect us to have a good time. These really were going to be years of freedom, weren't they?

I sat down and took a few sips of the cool, fizzy liquid. Stuck above the table was a giant pin board. The only things it presently contained were an 'In the case of Fire' notice and the Freshers' timetable. Every evening was jam packed. I spotted another notice above the microwave. It had three sections with step by step instructions on how to use the kettle, microwave and toaster. After the last section there was even a 'handy tips!' section including *'Do not butter your bread until after it is toasted.'* This was messily highlighted in yellow by some previous fresher. I shared his supposed sense of incongruity. They'd also underlined the instruction for the kettle, *'Do not put the tea bags in the kettle but make up in a mug.'* The Bristol logo was proudly in the corner.

"And some people were worried they wouldn't get in," smiled Mike, reading my expression.

"I'm not sure which worries me more; that the Uni thinks we might not know not to put metal in the microwave, or that some people genuinely need that. Who's never made a cup of tea?"

Mike grinned. "God forbid what we might do with the oven. No instructions here!"

I laughed and started to feel better. Mike wandered over to grab a box from the table and glanced up at the large, empty board.

"There's a history night in Lizard Lounge on Friday night. I'm game for it if you want to come?"

I nodded. So many new people to meet and nobody I could just be myself with yet. "Sure." I stood and picked up a box of saucepans. "Is there an order to the cupboards?"

Mike shrugged, so I put my things in various sensible places, and then tried to squeeze the bread and milk my mum had got me into an already full fridge.

Soon Chloe came around and ushered us all out of the flat for the Hall meeting. We meandered to the bar in a tight group. Holly turned out to have a sweet freckled face and bright red hair. She was wearing black eyeliner and I longed to tell her brown would suit her better. She was already chatting to Anna. I felt a sudden surge of panic that I wasn't getting on that well with anyone, and then tried to suppress my nerves in case they stopped me from appearing confident, and easy to be with.

We filed into the chairs in the bar and I tried to start a conversation with the guy beside me. Anna sat the other side, still asking Holly questions about her boyfriend and I felt ignored. The guy had blond curly hair and looked quite young and seemed engrossed in a leaflet he was holding. He had a disarming posture which helped me build up my courage.

"Hi, I'm Izzy," I tried.

He looked up and smiled warmly. "Josh. Please forgive me if I forget your name, there's so many new faces."

"Likewise," I smiled.

He put the leaflet in his pocket. "You settling in all right, Izzy?"

I shrugged. "I think I'm getting there. My flat seems nice. And yourself?"

"Well I'm a second year so it's a bit different for me. It's weird that all the people are different. I'd got used to associating this place with the same old people." He looked around wistfully.

"Why did you stay a second year, to be on the JCR?"

"Kind of. I'm actually here as a CU rep."

"What's that?" I asked starting to feel a bit overwhelmed by all this new information I was supposed to know.

"It's er... the Christian Union. Each Hall has three or four people chosen by the main CU to run smaller Hall CUs and to help support people. Many of us choose to live in so we can get to know you guys better."

"Oh," I said, feeling strange. I hadn't really expected to find Christians at Uni. Especially not in some strange organisation. Did he really believe like Sarah had? I felt like I had so many questions, but was it safe to ask them? I had the feeling that most of the questions weren't really meant to be asked and had no answers. You were just meant to *believe* and *have faith* and all that cheesy jazz. "So, who are the other second years here?"

Josh pointed out the JCR president, the guy in charge of hall events and then a second CU rep, Fran. All I could see of her was straight black hair.

The Warden then stood up and made a speech about the importance of work, the dangers of smoking, being sensible and about keeping things tidy. It made me feel like a young teenager all over again. Then the JCR president gave a speech about nothing at all. The evening activity was a beach themed evening in the bar. I wondered if 'beach themes' existed just to create a socially acceptable situation for girls to just wear bikinis and guys to show off their abs indoors. Sounded a bit silly to me, I wanted to dress up not down, but this world was so new to me and I had no idea what was the normal 'cool' thing. Who knew, maybe people came as lobsters and palm trees. A bit late to sort out a costume now though.

Next it was Josh's turn to nervously introduce himself and Fran. They invited us all to a very civilised sounding afternoon tea and cake tomorrow. I wondered who went to such events. Christians? People who liked religion? People who liked that sort of mild social scene? I wondered if you would just be innocently munching on carrot cake when a deep philosophical or entirely personal question would be thrown at you. No escape! I smiled to myself.

When he sat back down and the Warden dismissed us, Anna reached over me to touch Josh on the knee. "Hi," she said. "I think we spoke on Facebook."

Josh smiled warmly. "I remember, it's Anna, isn't it? Shall we expect you tomorrow?"

Anna nodded. "Definitely. It's so nice to know you guys are here."

I awkwardly looked between them, sitting as far back in my chair as I could, and was relieved when everyone stood to go back to their flats. So was Anna a Christian too?

We wandered back together to cook and chaos commenced. Mike and Fred were already arguing over the identity of some food cans. I realised somebody had identical saucepans to me and struggled to remember which stack was mine. I'd brought a massive bag of pasta and some bottles of sauce to last me until I could go food shopping, but there wasn't much space for the opened jar in the fridge next to Mike's beers. Did he really have to chill so many at once?

Chloe started to pull out all the contents of the cupboards without permission saying we should start again with a labelling system and ordered Mike to stack his beers on the tiny fire escape balcony. Anna just smiled her disarming, get-along-with-everyone smile and Holly sat away by herself as if nothing involved her. My stuff was suddenly back all over the floor and half my flatmates were cross. I'd never felt so alone in my life.

Chapter Five

Freshers' week rushed by in a confusing blur of faces, names and courses. Some nights were fun, some were awkward. In all of them I stuck with Chloe, Holly and Anna in an almost desperate friendship. There were already a hundred and fifty photos of us together on Facebook and I'd sent a load to be printed so I could stick them up on the kitchen board. Holly and Anna weren't as keen on clubbing as the rest of us so often went back early. By then Chloe and I were almost too drunk to notice and Mike and Fred were there to walk us home or catch a taxi. I'd already spent a night holding Chloe's hair back as she vomited into our loo.

By the time Friday night came I was exhausted but excited to finally meet my course mates in a social environment. These at last would be the people I needed to know. Anna and Holly were at a medic's bar crawl. Anna had spent a whole afternoon worrying about how notorious they could be. I had thought she was being a bit over dramatic. She always left early anyway and barely drank.

It was just going to be me and Mike and I wasn't sure what I felt about that. He tended to go off and socialise with others whenever we went anywhere as a flat. However, he was always a good laugh and I had to admit I enjoyed watching him when he was animated with his mates.

I decided to go for more dramatic make-up than usual and make more of a statement, the 'anything goes' effect of Freshers' making me bold. I wore a small cream dress that had diamond cut outs at the hips, stomach and chest making it very sexy. I wore massive sparkling heels and shoved flats in my tiny handbag for the walk through hilly Bristol. I hadn't realised how easy I'd had it at home with the gentle inclines I'd always complained about. As I gave myself one last look in the mirror I felt the sickening mix of wavering confidence in my appearance with the desperate desire to be liked. I glanced up at a photo of Sarah, smiled at her and then banged on Mike's door to interrupt his video game.

Mike grinned as he looked me up and down. "Looking good, Izzy," he grinned.

"Not too shabby yourself," I laughed, tugging playfully on the collar of his Calvin Klein shirt, stretched too tight across his broad chest.

The bar was supposed to be more 'quirky' and 'alternative' but to me every place just looked dark and crowded. The only feature that seemed to make a difference was the price of the drinks. For the first half of the evening I felt an enormous pressure to remember everyone and make a positive impression. These strangers were my year. I tried to smile and hug and pose for as many group photos as I could in case people didn't remember me. However, by the time I'd had two pints of cider and a large glass of red, I decided that I wouldn't care anymore. I was there to enjoy myself after all.

I searched through the crowded bar, pushing between unsteady people and trying to help my feet avoid stilettos, and went over to the small dance floor looking for Mike. He was the only guy I knew at all, so would be the least exhausting to be around. I saw him dancing with a very drunk girl with long brown hair. For some inexplicable reason I felt a stab of jealousy and swayed over to the pair, pretending to be slightly more drunk than I was. I *needed* Mike. He was the only one I knew.

I rested my hand on his shoulder and turned him to make the dance three way. The music was quieter than a true club but the remixes were good. There were ones to sing along to and pretend you knew every single word, and ones which were almost pure rhythm. I felt myself unwind and relax. Felt myself releasing the stress of meeting so many people. Of losing Sarah.

I got more and more into the music and started to deliberately out dance the other girl, wanting to win Mike over to me. She was drunk and uncoordinated anyway. Mike got closer to me and I felt my heart starting to race in affirmation and expectation. I felt beautiful and sexy. He wrapped his arms around my waist and I smiled at him.

I wanted him to kiss me. But part of me wasn't sure that I wanted him to. We were flatmates, right? Friends? But then I wanted that buzz, the heat, the excitement and the feeling that he found me beautiful. In the heat and through the drink it was hard to think clearly of anything but the excitement of having him close.

His head moved lower to mine. Sweat was dripping from his over waxed hair but he smelt of nice cologne. He paused as if waiting for my permission. He slowed his dance and I moved up to kiss him. A thrill rushed through me as he gently moved his lips around mine. Then we parted and I eyed him, flushed and happy, yet nervous.

"Nothing too fast, yes?" I yelled over the music.

He grinned. "Doesn't have to mean anything unless you want it to, babe."

I smiled and then turned to find one of the few seats that wasn't taken up by people who were half passed out. I took off my shoes and rubbed my feet. '*Doesn't have to mean anything...*' I mulled it over. See, it was just like I'd told Sarah. Sex and kissing didn't need to mean anything but the thrill. Yet at the same time I was upset that he hadn't felt anything behind it. Of course he didn't. We'd barely had a sober conversation! It had only been a spur of the moment thing. Then again he'd said '*unless you want it to...*' did that mean he wanted us to become a couple? Or just go further and sleep together?

Suddenly I felt very tired and slightly sick. I checked my phone for the time. 3am. There was a text from Anna as well. I opened it up in surprise. '*Hope u guys hav had a gd time 2night. Be safe. Let me know when ur back. xxx.*' I read it again and again. It was exactly the sort of text Sarah would have written. One that was overly concerned for my safety, like you'd expect from your mum. For a split second I could imagine she was alive again and was just waiting for me in our Durdham flat. I shook myself. Stupid drink was making me all emotional and overly imaginative.

A guy, who'd previously introduced himself as Harry, was carrying four glasses of water and gave me one with a wink as he passed. I drank it gratefully and watched the rest of my year, noting who was getting with whom so I could relate to the gossip the term was sure to start with. One guy had randomly stripped to his boxers and was dancing harder than everyone on the dance floor. Around him girls were flashing cameras like the paparazzi. I zoned out for a period and then Mike made me jump by putting his hand on my shoulder.

"You ready to go, Izzy?" his words were slightly slurred, his smile lopsided.

I nodded and smiled. "Sounds like a plan."

Mike had already got two other Durdhamite girls waiting by the door, I couldn't remember their names, and together we staggered into a waiting taxi. I sat in the middle and, without really thinking, rested my head on Mike's shoulder. He put his arm around me and for the first time since Sarah's death, I felt safe and secure. I felt valued again.

*

I woke up at 12.30pm with a headache. After thirty minutes I managed to motivate myself to get up, get a drink and have a nice long shower. As I walked back to my room in just a towel, Chloe burst out of her room with a squeal. "Izzy! Hard night last night? Enjoy it?" She mimicked a prolonged kiss.

I felt my stomach knot. "What are you talking about?"

She grabbed my hand and pulled me into her room where her apple mac lay on her bed. I clutched my towel as it flapped and was glad none of the boys were around. There on Facebook was a picture of Mike and I kissing, our faces bleached in the flash. I didn't recognise the name of the person who had posted it, but he had tagged Mike. The caption read, '*So the saliva tree continues*!'

"People need to grow up," I grumbled, starting to comb my wet hair with my hands. "It was just a kiss."

"Well it was two for Mike!" said Chloe, flicking to the next picture in Mike's photos. It showed him kissing the drunken brunette he'd been dancing with earlier. The caption said '*So the saliva tree begins*! *The sluts and man-whores of our year revealed*!'

I froze and Chloe caught my expression and put her hand to her mouth. "Sorry, Izzy, I kinda assumed you knew." She stood up and put a hand on my shoulder. "Sorry, that was mean of me. You actually like him, don't you?"

"It was just a kiss," I repeated angrily. "That doesn't make me a slut." I turned and slammed my way into my room. Chloe was trying to shout that it wasn't referring to me.

I dressed to try to distract myself from tears and then did my make-up. My anger helped me focus instead of breaking down. It wasn't fair. People were always encouraging you to enjoy yourself, kiss and sleep with whoever you like. However, when you just did what everyone else did you were suddenly a whore or a slut or easy. Why couldn't they make up their minds? I threw my hairbrush onto my bed in frustration and counted to ten as Mum had always done. Then I went to Mike's door and knocked on it. I did it without thinking or I knew I'd never have the courage and would spend the rest of the day sulking.

There was the sound of some drawers opening and closing and then Mike appeared in t-shirt and trackies. His hair was mussed up in a surprisingly attractive way which lessened my anger slightly, but let my tears get closer to the surface.

"Izzy," he said. "Looking beautiful even while hung over."

"More beautiful than the other girl?" I bit. "Which one of us was the better kisser?"

He looked taken aback. "Well you actually. Why are you so mad? I'd be an idiot to turn any of you beautiful ladies down. I didn't lie or anything. I'm single; it's what you do when you're single."

I opened my mouth but no come-back came. Our moment was meant to have been special. The climax of an evening. He wasn't meant to have kissed other girls. But then again, it wasn't like we were dating or anything. I felt like an idiot.

"Izzy," said Mike gently, "I'm sorry if I hurt you. Tammy started kissing me earlier. I had no idea I would later kiss you.

It was just my way of saying I find you attractive. To be fair it was the first time you'd shown me any attention, and you kinda started it."

I looked at my feet and shifted them awkwardly. So it had been meaningless. He had just kissed anybody who let him.

Mike put a finger beneath my chin and lifted me up to his face. I noticed for the first time his eyes were a bright green. "Would you forgive me, Izzy, if I took you out to dinner tonight and behaved more like a gentleman?"

A surge of excitement covered over my grief. My first date in years. I blushed, grateful that he wasn't just letting me be the overreacting idiot. "That would be nice, thanks."

Mike smiled. "Don't expect anything too fancy, mind. You know compared with how sexy you are when you dance you're actually quite sweet and innocent when you're sober."

I bit my lip. "There are photos on Facebook calling us sluts and man-whores."

To my surprise Mike laughed and shook his head. "Don't worry, it's only a joke. I'll see you at 7.30pm." He grinned and closed the door.

I skipped back to my room and then changed my mind and burst into Chloe's instead.

"We're going on a date," I squealed. "Mike just asked me out to dinner!"

Chloe made a very high-pitched sound and clapped her hands together. She jumped up and hugged me. "That's great! Where you going? You guys didn't hang around at all did you? What you going to wear?"

Maybe University was enjoyable and exciting after all.

*

Durdham was in the centre of a cluster of University Halls in Stoke Bishop. Most of the other Halls were in Clifton, which was much closer to most of the lecture theatres. There was a friendly rivalry between both groups. However, there was a subtler rivalry between the Stoke Bishop Halls themselves. Wills Hall was the brunt of most of the jokes, being by far the most expensive and grand. The favourite saying was 'The Wills on the bus go ra ra ra.' which I didn't really think was as clever as everyone gave it credit for. Durdham sat comfortably in the middle both in location and cost, making it nicely immune to most of the jokes. Most people saw it as the quiet Hall, especially since we were divided into flats and had no communal dining. UH was the other extreme and sat at the bottom of the hill. However, despite how the place looked, it had a fun reputation of partying and community. The Stoke Bishop Halls seemed to be much closer to one another than the Clifton Halls. I assumed that was because out here in the suburbs there was less local entertainment, so we visited each other's bars constantly. We also walked to lectures in massive amalgamations of Halls and subjects since we were further away. Each Clifton Hall was more independent.

Stoke Bishop was right next to a large expanse of grass called 'The Downs'. This plain but pretty park often seemed to separate us from the whole world. And not in a good way. You had to walk through it to get anywhere. The main University buildings were a forty minute walk in total; first across The Downs and then there was the massive, busy hill of Whiteladies Road. All the shops and clubs and bars were the other side of the Downs, behind us the northern suburbs felt more like a village than a city. It was one thing in the daytime, when the expanse of grass was full of picnics and dogs and people doing various sports, but they were notorious at night.

We were constantly told not to walk across them alone in the dark whether girl or boy and to stick to the road if possible, where the only lights were. Rumours circulated about them a plenty during Freshers' but nobody seemed to actually *know* anyone who'd got hurt.

That evening, however, I was glad The Downs were there, as it gave Mike and me a good thirty minutes' walk to chat before reaching the quirky burger bar he had chosen on Whiteladies Road, the centre of the Freshers' universe. It was so much easier to talk when walking alongside somebody with the view to look at, than awkwardly staring across at them when you barely knew each other.

I felt pretty in a casual yellow summer dress that was only a tad too cold for the October evening, and a white cardigan. Mike smelled powerfully of aftershave. I had decided not to brave heels as my feet were still very sore from the previous night but I tried not to limp like an idiot. I was so excited I could barely think straight. What sort of things did you do and say to come across as normal on your first date?

"So, where you from?" asked Mike.

I gave him a sideways look. "Cambridgeshire. You already knew that. And you're from Hampshire. Everyone seems to be from Hampshire or London."

"Ha, I'd forgotten. You apply for Cambridge then?"

"No. I barely gave it a thought. A lot of stuff happened around my A-levels so I didn't really do any extra stuff or aim deliberately high."

"What stuff?"

I shrugged. "Rubbish stuff."

Mike put his arm around me. "You know you're one of the most secretive people I know. Trying to get information from you is even difficult when you're drunk."

"My best friend died in a car accident." The mood was suddenly destroyed.

"Oh. Izzy, I'm sorry, I didn't mean to bring something like that up. But... thanks for telling me." He gave me a look that made my chest tighten. He was becoming better looking every time I saw him. This could really work.

I talked about my brother and mum. He told me about his parents and sisters. We talked a little about school but then the conversation started to dry up.

We walked in silence down the top of Whiteladies watching locals and students milling around the local pubs.

"What do you want to do with your life?" I said suddenly.

Mike shrugged. "I want to get into publishing or something similar. Or maybe review articles for a newspaper, or whatever."

"I mean more long term. Like your whole life." I spread my arms out and twirled in a little circle, trying to seem fun.

He raised an eyebrow at me. "Er, what made that question come out?" He paused for a moment. "Have a good career; earn enough money to get a nice place. Eventually get married and have a few kids. Have some sort of impact on the world and then retire and live on a yacht with my model wife." He grinned at me. "Why, you imagining our life together?" He laughed and elbowed me.

I smiled. "No, no, of course not. I've just been thinking too much recently. What is life actually about? They say money and fame can't bring happiness, but everyone still fights for it. It just all seems... empty. It makes me wonder what I'm working towards. An unhappy life like my mum's? And then we just die..."

Mike grinned and wrapped his arm around my shoulders, "Bloody Hell, Izzy, you sure you're not meant to be studying philosophy. People are only meant to speak like that when drunk. Dates are meant to be fun."

I shook myself. Idiot! I needed to come across as beautiful and funny and sexy. That's what Mike would want. I needed to be happy. My brain just went funny places after thinking about Sarah's death. Embarrassed, I smiled up at my flatmate. "Sorry, Mike. How long to this place anyway?"

"Five minutes. Izzy it's downhill!" I realised his arm was still around my shoulders. I needed to fill my mind with happy thoughts. Mike was good looking, tall and sporty. His image said good things about me being his girlfriend. If we were boyfriend and girlfriend... He seemed kind. He certainly made me laugh and feel secure. People would think twice before taking him on in a dark alleyway.

We didn't talk that much in the burger bar due to how massive the burgers were. They took all my concentration to eat without getting sauce all over my face and dress. As it was I had to have an emergency loo trip when some bacon fell into my bra. I was so aware of Mike's eyes upon me and wanted him to see I was good enough. I wanted the excitement of this relationship. I wanted to feel whole, not broken.

On the walk back we were feeling more comfortable with each other and talked about light-hearted nonsense. We held hands. We laughed at drunken people. As it got dark it was clear my dress and cardigan weren't adequate so he wrapped his coat around my shoulders. As we got to the other side of The Downs he slipped his arm around my waist. I automatically sucked my tummy in.

At last we stopped outside the flat door and kissed. It was a long deep kiss that made my stomach freeze and my body on edge. Mike tasted of onion and beer but I didn't care. Then he winked at me, took a step back and opened the flat door. As soon as it closed behind us the kitchen door opened and three curious heads popped around to study us. I laughed and they awkwardly backed off not sure whether to call us to join them or leave us be. Chloe winked at me before leaving the kitchen door open using the bin behind her as a doorstop.

I turned to Mike, slipping his coat from my shoulders. "Thanks for a nice evening." I suddenly felt very awkward again. Seemed it was catching.

But Mike confidently grinned, tucked a strand of hair behind my ear and then walked to his room. I stood uncertain in the hall for a few minutes looking between my bedroom, his bedroom and the sitting room. Eventually I decided to just go to the bathroom. It sounded like a film had just ended next door anyway. I caught a glimpse of Fred dangling himself out of the window to smoke. You could still smell it in the flat. We'd better not get told off for that. Sure enough Chloe started shouting at him to take it outside.

That night I could barely sleep. I couldn't get Mike out of my head. The feel of his hand in mine or around my shoulders. The look he'd given me once or twice which had made my body flush with heat. His broad back. His floppy hair and bright green eyes. I re-enacted the kiss. Then I started to imagine it had gone further. My heart raced. I felt like I was on the verge of something exciting, some grand self-discovery. Maybe this relationship would be the start of me truly experiencing life. Everyone was obsessed with dating and sex. It was meant to be the best thing in life. Apart from maybe Sarah who'd seen it as precious but had wanted to lock it up. Almost as if it were dangerous.

It was light outside when I finally fell asleep. I was woken by somebody knocking on the door. I groggily checked my watch. 1pm. How could I still feel tired? I was dreading getting up for lectures next morning even though the first one was 10am. I flopped back onto my pillow.

"Izzy?" came Chloe's voice.

"Come in," I croaked. "But no boys. I'm in my pyjamas." And probably looked a state.

Chloe excitedly came in and bounced onto my bed. I was surprised to see her long hair was actually quite wavy. She'd brought hair straighteners with her and proceeded to heat them up while asking me a hundred questions about our date.

I laughed and gave her an outline. I asked if everyone else was up. I really meant Mike but didn't want to sound like one of those weird people who shut all their friends off when they got a boyfriend.

"Mike and Fred went out to play football with this unofficial club. They left about an hour ago. Holly went to the library to work. Work! Can you believe it? Term's not even started properly yet. Apparently she sometimes skypes her boyfriend just so that they can *work* together. And Anna, strangely enough, went to church. Said she was going to go to a few today to 'try them out.' Can't believe they can be that different. Not that I've ever been."

I paused, my eyes involuntarily flicking up to photos of Sarah on my wall. "Anna goes to church?"

Chloe nodded. "Yeah. When she said she was a Christian, she actually meant it. That's why she didn't drink or kiss anyone or anything. Well at least she's not been trying to convert us. Can you imagine how annoying and awkward that would be?"

I smiled half-heartedly but my stomach felt twisted. It was like a strange joke of fate. Lose one Christian, gain another. It was like life was taunting me. You can never have Sarah back, but I'll give you somebody to constantly remind you what she was like. You'll never get over her.

"Izzy?" asked Chloe, studying my face, unsure if she'd offended. For a split second I saw in her a mirror of my own insecurities. We all so desperately wanted to be liked in this new world.

I smiled. "Sorry, Chloe. An old friend was a Christian back home, that's all. The real, crazy sort. I miss her."

Chloe nodded, still uncertain, but eager to move on. She started to change the subject as I said, "Have you ever thought Christianity might be true?"

She looked at me strangely and tucked her straightened hair out of the way to reach the bottom layer that was still wavy. "Come on, Izzy, of course it's not. People used to believe in God so that the world made sense, but science explains it now. There's no need for a God to explain things."

I nodded. That made sense. "But then why do people still believe in God? Anna's a scientist after all. Sarah was as well. She wanted to be a doctor too. Neither's stupid."

Chloe shrugged. "It makes people feel happy to think somebody is watching over them and that they're not going to truly die. It's a coping mechanism that works for some, not others. Makes the world seem less scary."

I stared out of the window. "That's what I used to tell Sarah." Looking back I realised how immediately defensive I'd been every time. I'd seen it as her telling me I was wrong, so I'd hit back hard. I'd not liked her disapproving of how I acted or dressed, even when she never said anything. I'd seen her views as unreasonable; therefore I'd never really addressed them.

Chloe took my hand, concerned. "You all right, Izzy? Everyone thinks differently. That's a good thing. Nothing to worry about."

I was doing it again, turning the mood sour. I needed to stop doing that or everyone would just feel depressed around me. I smiled. "So, Chloe, you found any boys you like yet? You said you were single. Any recent history?"

Chloe smiled and relaxed; the conversation on familiar territory again. "I had two boyfriends at school. Both lasted about a year. I broke them both off when I wanted to move on. I wasn't in love or anything, it's just nice to have one, you know? I'm keeping an eye out for a casual relationship. I don't see the point of getting serious until after Uni."

I nodded. Seemed to make sense. "So you don't get too close? Just enjoy their company?"

"Yeah. Though more than just their company," she laughed and winked. "You express things very innocently sometimes, Izzy. I move on when it becomes inconvenient. For example, I wasn't up for doing a long distance relationship with James as he's in Uni in Manchester. *So far away*! I'll put the work in when it's serious." She put down her hair straighteners and flicked her hair back. "How about you? What's your story?"

I blushed, slightly embarrassed. "I had a boyfriend when I was fourteen for a few months. Was all a bit awkward to be honest. We just didn't get on very well. Nothing but a few kisses since."

Chloe looked shocked. "*Nothing*? No wonder you sound so innocent. With that boy, did you ever sleep with him?"

"Of course not, I was fourteen!" I was uncomfortable with her bluntness.

"Izzy, you are missing out. You need to get in on this. It's the twenty first century." She spoke as if her views were universally agreed upon.

I looked down at the duvet. Why did everyone sound so confident with what was the right thing to do except me?

"Though, Izzy, seriously now." Chloe took both of my

hands and looked in my eyes. "Don't let anyone pressurise you into anything and be safe. Some boys like it if you keep them waiting a month or two. Builds up the tension, you know? I don't think I could have ever waited that long." She sighed. "Make life serve you, Izzy. Grab it by the throat and stop over thinking. Just do what makes you happy as long as it doesn't hurt anyone and, well, be happy!"

Chapter Six

Monday came around quickly. The lectures were all boring introductions about how important the course was and our degree and how to do well. I sat next to Mike who lounged back in his chair and made no note of the deadlines.

I barely recognised anyone from the night out and tried to talk to as many people as possible and put them in friendship groups in my head. The only one who had really stuck from amongst the blur was Harry who had handed me the water. He seemed to be 'the nice guy' that absolutely everyone seemed to know already. How had he managed to talk to so many people? I decided to hone my efforts and concentrated on mentally dividing my course mates into people like me and not like me so I could fit in quickly. They all seemed very friendly and very different from the stereotypical groups at school. This seemed a much more tolerant world.

I got to know the other two Durdhamite historians from the walk to and from Halls, Kyla and Jess. They were inseparable. One was half Asian with long black curls and massive blue eyes, the other had a short brown crop and a large, hard mouth. Both were shy and quiet. Others from the Stoke Bishop Halls walked with us as well if they happened to have lectures that coincided. I seemed to be in constant groups and crowds. All in all as the days slipped by I was spending a lot of time with Mike, but none of it private or with room to talk.

Chloe had organised a cooking rota once she'd realised Fred was eating pasta and tomato sauce or pot noodles every night. She demanded rather than offered to teach him to cook and even colour coded the rota, sticking it as the first new item to the giant cork board. It was nice to only have to cook once a week, even if Mike and Fred put minimal effort in their first meal. Nobody had much experience and yet everyone was so opinionated. '*Freeze the onion first then you won't cry.*' '*No, you just need to leave the skin on until the last bit.*' '*Take the skin off; just don't cut the ends off until you've finished the slicing.*' '*Boil the water in the kettle before putting it in the saucepan to speed it up.*' '*No, don't use the kettle; it's more expensive as it uses lots of electricity.*'

The arguments were just annoying and Chloe often seemed to care too much whereas Anna would try to say them in a helpful way that I still found annoying. I tried to make sure I was the only one in the kitchen while cooking. I had a few recipes up my sleeve already since I'd often cooked for Jack and myself when Mum had been out on dates or girls' nights. I'd also been given a ridiculous amount of cook books from family friends in the last six months. However, so many of them included things I'd never heard of. What was 'cumin', or 'harissa paste'? Where did you get molasses from? How much shopping should you get without a car? When was Sainsbury's Basics range fine and when was it not worth it? Being an adult was already feeling a bit more complicated than I expected and that wasn't even taking into account the ridiculous amounts of paperwork I was accumulating and trying to file responsibly. I had no idea what any of the long bank letters about '*changes to your account*' meant or if normal people actually read them. I wasn't sure which letters you threw away and which ones you kept, so I just kept them all in my 'bank' file, which was steadily starting to overtake my 'student finance' file with its ridiculously repetitive letters, all of which I was too scared to bin. Better safe than sorry.

My cooking day was Tuesday and I spent a good two hours shopping, and walking home with the bags, then a further hour cooking before serving my mum's lasagne recipe a lot later than I'd expected. Mike was out Wednesday afternoon with the football team who then went clubbing in the evening. He also practised on Thursday. By Friday afternoon I was feeling like our relationship was slipping away into just flatmates again and wasn't sure how to stop it. '*Make life serve you, Izzy. Grab it by the throat and stop over thinking.*' That's what Chloe had said and she always seemed so in control. I needed to take matters into my own hands.

We didn't have any lectures after eleven as we were meant to be reading for a practice essay. I'd spent a few hours in the library until lunch, but I just couldn't get Mike out of my head. I'd borrowed a massive book on women's rights in the forties and now slogged back to Durdham with it in my arms. I entered with difficulty, half balancing the book on my knee as I fumbled with keys and door handles, and then dumped it straight on my bed in exhaustion, unopened. I slumped down and stretched my sore arms back and forth. After my breathing had levelled and my computer was starting to load, I realised I could hear music coming from Mike's room next door. I stood up and tried to contain my excitement. At last an afternoon we could have on our own.

I changed into a more revealing top and brushed up a carefully calculated level of make-up to give a reasonably natural look. I left the heavy book and knocked on Mike's door. No answer. I pushed it open cautiously and saw him studying at the other side of the room, speakers blaring in his ears. He seemed to be reading book reviews rather than the books themselves on his computer screen.

"Mike?" I called across the music.

He spun around in his chair in surprise and then grinned. I really did like his grin. "Sorry, Izz, was the music too loud for you?"

"Not at all. I was just wondering if we could, you know, spend some time together?"

He smiled and pulled my arm so that I fell into his lap. My constant thoughts about him for the last week had built up this moment so that it felt so important, one I needed to not mess up. They also meant my heart and stomach were going crazy so I couldn't think straight. Before I could think of what to say his lips were pressed on mine and one hand pushed the small of my back. The other became tangled in my hair. All my senses sharpened. I could feel my entire body. All the places we touched. Chloe was right. Nothing else brought this crazy, powerful rush of emotion. I was missing out.

After a few minutes his lips moved to my chin, then down to my neck. The more he kissed me, the more I wanted him to go further. My whole body ached.

Then he stopped, leaving my skin burning. He grinned. "Would you like to go for milkshakes, sexy lady?"

I was too breathless and confused to do anything other than nod. He had stopped so suddenly. Didn't he want to go further? But then again, now that I was starting to regain cognitive function, I wasn't sure I wanted to go further yet. I barely knew him.

We spent the afternoon together walking to and from the

milkshake shop and relaxing on the Downs in the October sun, admiring the fiery glory of the autumn colours in the trees. The whole time he kept smiling at me. His hand was always on my hip or shoulder. Once or twice he even laid it on my bum. I felt amazing. At last I had all of his attention. When sitting on The Downs we kissed deeply when nobody was close, giggling when we spotted dog walkers appearing around the trees. Then as it started to get darker he grew bolder and kissed me even when people were walking or jogging by.

We came home to find dinner almost ready. Holly was doing a stir fry. I was almost cross for the interruption but I told myself to stop being silly. I sat next to Mike and he frequently rested his hand on my knee and then thigh under the table all the way through the meal. I was so distracted I couldn't join in the conversations. I just smiled and nodded along. The more Mike touched me the more my body burned for it. I could barely stand the tension. My mouth was so dry I had to sip water with almost every mouthful.

After washing up to some cheesy pop music, Anna went to the flat of some Durdhamites she'd met through CU. Chloe was going out clubbing with course mates. Holly wanted an early night as she was visiting her boyfriend in Exeter tomorrow. Fred had a friend around and death metal music was up loud in his room so I didn't know why Holly was even attempting to sleep. We were pretty much on our own.

"Movie?" asked Mike.

I smiled, my brain felt fuzzy and impulsive. I almost felt drunk. I would do anything he suggested.

He set up the laptop on his bed and we snuggled up together to watch one of the Matrix films in the dark. I could barely concentrate as Mike started by stroking my back then gradually started to lift my top up, stroking my bare skin, higher and higher up my back. It reached a point about thirty minutes in when I couldn't take it any longer. Mike's hand was almost at my bra strap so I turned around so his hand landed directly on my chest. He pressed on the material of my bra and we started to kiss, the Matrix forgotten and the sounds of shooting covering up our heavy breathing.

Suddenly there was a loud bang across the corridor. We both paused for a second, and then he moved his mouth down to my neck again. There was another bang followed by some loud swearing and shouting.

Mike swore. "Keep thinking those thoughts, Izzy, I'll be right back."

He stumbled out of bed into the corridor. More shouting and swearing. The sound of somebody slamming the front door. Mike opened his door again and light flooded in. "Izzy, phone an ambulance. Fred's taken something that idiot brought with him." He held a small clear bag in his hand.

I froze in shock and then rushed past Mike into Fred's room. He was on the floor unconscious. He was foaming around the mouth and his hands were twitching. There was blood on his ear. I swore.

Mike grabbed me with both shoulders and led me out of the room. "Izzy, listen to me. Get an ambulance here and guide them in. I'll get him in the recovery position and make sure he doesn't vomit. Say it's an emergency."

For the first time in my life I dialled '999' and shakily talked to the operator. By the time I was begging for an ambulance to come quickly, I was in tears. *No, he wasn't conscious, yes he was breathing, no his eyes were closed, no I didn't know what he had taken, I don't know, I don't know, please just come, come now, please.* Today had been too much of an emotional rollercoaster.

I hurried to the car park entrance to help wave in the ambulance. It was there in fifteen minutes. The police came too. After we were back in the flat I stayed out of the way and let Mike do the talking. I was so glad he seemed to know just what to do. The police took a statement from me and then I was ignored but I felt glued in position in the corridor. Fred was taken out in a stretcher to hospital and Mike went with him.

I explained what was going on to Holly who stood, confused in her dressing gown, watching events. Then I went to bed. How could Fred be so stupid as to take that stuff? I covered my head under the covers and cried and cried.

At 2am my phone buzzed. I grabbed it hoping of news from Mike. But it was a text from Chloe saying she was spending the night with course mates and not to worry. I didn't feel like texting back what was happening so just sent her a kiss.

I drifted in and out of sleep until the loud front door woke me again. I checked my watch. 5am. I heard Mike's door open and close. He must have spent hours in hospital with Fred, he must be exhausted.

I quickly brushed my hair and hurried into his room. Mike had collapsed onto his bed fully dressed, an arm across his eyes. The Matrix film was still paused on his pillow. I'd forgotten to turn it off.

"Mike? You all right? How's Fred?"

"Izzy," he mumbled, sitting up. "You're meant to be in bed. Fred's still unconscious but they think he's okay. He has to have all these fluids going into him as he was very dehydrated so will be in hospital a few days. The police want to talk to his friend, whoever he was."

I squeezed Mike's hand. "I think you've done a great job. It was kind of you to spend that long with him."

Mike smiled at me tiredly. "Of course I had to. I wanted to know he was safe. Then it took a while to find a taxi. The doctors didn't want me there anyway. I was getting in the way. I'm... I'm sorry our evening was wrecked."

I smiled. "Wasn't your fault, Mike. I still had a nice time."

He cupped my chin and ran a finger down my cheek. "You're very beautiful, Izzy. Did you know that? And kind. I really like you. You know, *really* like you."

I blushed and laughed softly, the thrill of his words echoing inside me. I put a finger on his lips. "Hush, Mr Heath. You're talking rubbish."

He kissed my finger and then my hand and before I knew it, we were back to where we had been eight hours earlier.

*

I woke up next to Mike feeling strange and very tired. I was wedged between his back and the wall in the tiny single bed. He was still breathing heavily. I ached a lot down *there*. I felt like I had a lot of thoughts to process and was glad Mike was still asleep. I had thought it would be... different somehow. Everyone else said it was pure bliss and though it hadn't been unpleasant exactly, it certainly hadn't been ecstasy either. Mike's hands and lips had been wonderful. The excitement had been unbearable but what it had built up to had been, well, awkward and painful with nowhere to hide. I didn't really know what was normal for the first time. Everyone said there was blood and it could hurt but apart from that people just said they had an incredible time and hinted they were good in bed. Did anyone else ever have difficulty getting things to fit together? Would Mike think I was weird? Would he be put off by the strange noises I had made? I was so inexperienced, what if he wanted somebody better in bed? I'd never told him I'd been a virgin. Could I trust him with last night?

I calmed myself down. I needed reassurance that was all. I needed Mike to hug and kiss me, tell me I'm beautiful and sexy again. Then maybe, he could teach me to get better... when I wasn't so sore anyway.

Mike turned over in his sleep and I lifted his arm to snuggle underneath it. *This is all I need to be happy*, I told myself. Stop over thinking. Just be content.

Mike was still asleep thirty minutes later so I extracted myself and went back to my own bed. I slumped back onto the pillows. I wanted somebody to talk to, really talk to. Somebody who would tell me what's normal and what's right and wrong. I supposed that's one of the reasons you got a boyfriend. To be able to talk about deep stuff since it was so hard to find other people who you could talk to on that level and not be judged. But I didn't feel comfortable enough with Mike yet and didn't want him to know I was dissatisfied and a little scared. I'd talked to Sarah about deep stuff, but not *this stuff*. She had never understood me in this area.

I looked up at the photos of her on the wall and felt uncomfortable. I didn't want her watching me at the moment, I felt judged. I got up again and pulled the photos down and slid them under my computer. I ran a hand through my tangled hair and sighed. Things always felt better after a shower, I told myself.

*

For the rest of the afternoon I avoided thinking about Mike by looking into all the societies I could join. I'd been so overwhelmed at the Freshers' Fair that I'd only signed up to the 'Chocolate society' because they'd given out free chocolate, and the 'History Society' because I thought I probably should. Now I looked at the list on the website and the choice was huge. So many things I could do, experience, live through…

I looked through for a second time trying to narrow them down. I wanted one to help me keep fit and make friends and maybe compete in. I hesitated over something completely new like fencing, but I'd enjoyed being experienced and good at sport at school and feeling needed by my teammates. I decided to continue netball as I'd heard Bristol had a decent team and didn't have any of the kit I'd need for hockey. I emailed the captain and wrote 'Netball' on my timetable over Wednesday afternoons and Friday evenings.

A soft knock came at the door and Anna entered with a cupcake on a plate, still smelling fresh from the oven.

"Hey, Izzy, would you like a cake? I'm making them for my church small group tonight and have a few extra. Thought you could do with one after last night." She smiled and slipped the plate onto my desk.

I felt a lurch in my stomach. What did she know about how I felt about last night? Then common sense dawned and I realised she was talking about Fred. I pushed my chair back to face her. "Thanks, Anna, that's so kind. I've just been signing up for netball. You joined any of these societies?"

She sat down on my bed. "Just CU and a medic one. Didn't think I'd have enough time for much else with work so full on."

I took a bite of the warm sponge. "What's church small group?" I asked, curious.

"I meet up with some students and older people from my church every Saturday night. We talk about the sermon and read bits of the Bible."

"You must really love Christian stuff if you're doing that as well as church and the CU group here and all. Don't you get bored of talking about the same things over and over?"

Anna looked a little uncomfortable as if struggling with her response. "I believe it's very important. And yes I do enjoy it. You should come along to Hall CU sometime and see what we talk about."

I shook my head, thinking about Mike. The last thing I wanted now was to be around people who'd disapprove of me. Things were complicated enough already. "I don't think the world makes sense with or without God. Bad things still happen, people still struggle," I mumbled.

Anna paused and I realised I'd ruined the conversation again. Why couldn't I just be as happy as everyone else? Why couldn't I just gloss over the bad in my life as well?

"God helped me make sense of a lot of things, Izzy. And one day promises that the bad things will end." She bit her lip. "I'm sorry I've always struggled to talk about this. You should ask Josh or Fran sometime."

I smiled in a noncommittal way and she left. I sighed and took a bigger bite of the cake, remembering I'd not eaten at all that day. Suddenly, I felt acutely alone and very far away from home. I missed my home bedroom and I really missed Mum. I missed Sarah and school and the way everything was set out for you.

Mike suddenly entered without knocking. He'd showered and I liked the way wet hair suited him. He smiled and I saw exactly how his lips moved his cheeks. He smelled fresh and masculine. I felt myself let go again of the things I'd been worrying about as he moved behind my chair and hugged me from behind, moving my hair so he could kiss my neck. I felt myself flush.

"The flat above are having a small party tonight. Wanna come with me?" His breath tickled my ear.

I noticed that from his angle he was looking straight down my top at my cleavage and suddenly felt awkward. I leaned forward so I could turn around and face him. He met me with a kiss. How had I been feeling alone? The attention felt so wonderful, the feeling of being needed and wanted. That constant tingle in my stomach when he was close.

"Of course I'll come. You want food first? I'll make us a meal this evening if you like?"

He grinned. "Sure. Party starts at eight so we'll head up at nine. Sounds like a plan." He frowned suddenly and reached for where a picture of Sarah was sticking out from under the computer. "Who's this?"

It was the picture we'd taken from the top of the big oak in the park with the view of the fields behind. Our blonde and brown hair was being mixed as it blew around us as we perched on the high branch. One of my hands was around her waist, the other on the camera. She was gripping the trunk and laughing through nerves. Our faces looked so alive, that's why I'd always loved that photo.

I snatched it back and put it back under my computer. "Just a friend. Doesn't matter."

He frowned at me. "You sure?" Then he held up his hands at my frown. "Peace, peace!" He laughed and flopped back on my bed.

I smiled and sat down beside him, resting my head on his shoulder. He stroked my arm. I relaxed and had another attempt at happiness.

"Like gold refined seven times."

Chapter Seven

I couldn't believe we had career lectures again and we were only in our first year. I felt like I'd only just recovered from being bombarded with them at school. That question over and over again; what are you going to do with your life? Mike was skiving. Somehow he seemed capable of blocking out all thoughts of the future and could assume it would all just fall into place.

I sighed as I looked down at the empty boxes of a work sheet we'd been given. *'What would you like to achieve from your career?'*

At school I'd never really thought about it since Sarah's death had seemed to make a mockery of it. What importance had jobs when you could just die without warning? But now I felt I needed to concentrate. My life would go on even though Sarah would never become a doctor. I had to live and whatever job I chose I was going to spend hours and hours of every day doing it. But it just seemed such an impossible question. *What should I do?* It was the first question anyone asked an adult after their name. How they labelled them. *'This is Mr Smith, he's a lawyer! This is Miss Jones; she just works in a café.'* The thing people used to define you and box you. It was your job that brought you respect, made your parents proud, and meant you could support your family. It was a huge proportion of your identity.

I'd voiced my concerns to Mike that morning and he'd laughed at me and said I was being ridiculous thinking about it like that. Why not just enjoy this time of no responsibility and so much spare time and freedom? Why burden myself unnecessarily? Everyone would find a job eventually and then if you didn't like it, you just changed.

I shook myself mentally and told myself to relax. '*What would you like to achieve from your career?*'

Fulfilment, happiness, financial comfort, something not too stressful, being able to work around a family. But surely everyone wanted an easy, well paid job in which they could change the world yet not get stressed? I tried to think more decisively. *Teamwork, involving communication both spoken and written.*

I read the next box. '*What could you be doing now to help you achieve your career prospects?*'

I chewed my pen end and leaned over to see what Jayne had written in her box next to me. '*Internship with publishing company arranged this summer, social chair for the history society, attending regular debate society events and aim to be on the team next year.*'

I swore at her internally then smiled when I met her eyes. I was starting to feel stressed and doodled around the box border as I thought. What would I like to do? What *could* I do? Where would I have to live?

My phone buzzed and I checked it under the writing shelf. It was from Mike and rather suggestive and I blushed before I could control myself. I glanced to my neighbours but no one was watching me. Jayne was too busy scribbling down her perfect plans, and Harry was joking to people the other side about how he'd had to ring his mother the first time he'd tried to use his Hall washing machines. I thanked the higher powers that the lecture theatre was relatively empty. I read it again, half flattered, half disapproving. Idly I wondered if we would still be together at graduation. Maybe we would share a flat together in London as we got our first jobs. That would be nice. I didn't want to have to face it all alone. Maybe with Chloe, Holly and Anna close by. Fred had only come back from hospital to pack before going home to take a year out. I didn't suppose I'd see him again.

Suddenly it was the end of lectures for lunch time; most of my boxes remained unfilled. Harry glanced at me, saw my worried face and gave my shoulder a squeeze and winked before leaving. Oh well, it's only first year, I tried to reassure myself. Everyone else just *seemed* confident. Lots of time left to decide what to commit my life to.

I grabbed my bag, shoved the notes in and then checked my watch. I had three hours before my next lecture. I knew I should go to the library to work and eat my packed lunch as I was behind in two of my essays but I knew Mike was still at the flat and if I caught the bus we could have at least an hour and a half in the flat together before both going to lectures. His text lingered in my mind.

I let myself be swept along with the crush, passing small talk with the rest of my year, before being hit with the shock of the late autumn cold. The Arts and Social Sciences library was close, and always warm. I hesitated, and then I spotted Anna on the other side of the road and shouted her name and waved. I hurried over and she grinned over her red scarf framed by her bright blonde hair.

"My brain's been fried by anatomy and physiology all

morning, Izz." She mimicked falling asleep. "Want to eat lunch with me? Holly's gone to the gym and abandoned me."

I paused then grinned. I hadn't spent much one on one time with Anna and it would be nice. "Go on then. The ASS library?"

She smiled. "Sure."

We turned around and walked against the busy flow of chattering students all bundled in layers of clothes against the cold and knocking each other with rucksacks and folders. I watched the pretty, grey Victorian houses as we passed them, looking for the signs which said which ones were owned by the university and thinking what it would be like to be a student in each department. Imagining all the different lives and passions and ambitions crammed together for three short years. So many beliefs, cultures and experiences. It seemed strange that such a short time could define your whole life.

Anna recognised a few people in the street and we ended up stopping three times as she introduced me to people from the CU or other medics. I still didn't quite understand how she knew so many people. She'd mentioned before that the whole CU was about three hundred strong, yet she seemed to know lots of them well already. They always seemed to be so happy to greet each other on the street and eager to chat whereas with most of my course mates or netball team I'd just smile or wave.

We reached the ASS library and found a seat in the café to eat our lunch, dumping our stuff before queuing for coffee. Anna briefly chatted to two people on a table across from us who seemed to be discussing something written in the Bible. Didn't they find that odd to do in public? Then again discussing ideas and exploring different opinions and beliefs was meant to be encouraged at University wasn't it?

We started our lunch and talked about course mates and

school friends and pets and the recent pranks that had been done in Durdham. However, I couldn't stop glancing at the two boys with the Bible. They looked alternatively serious and joyful. Then suddenly they started to pray. What a strange thing to do in a café. Why would they do that outside of church or their home? I wondered if they thought the same way as Anna. As Sarah.

"Do you pray every day?" I asked Anna suddenly. It seemed so strange after all those years when Sarah had tried to bring God into a conversation and I'd stopped her, that now it was me starting it.

She seemed caught off guard and shrugged slightly. "Well yes. I try to pray as often as I remember."

"What do you pray for?" I thought about Sarah's prayer diary and all the different people in it, including me, time after time. I took a bite of my apple, my mouth tingling at the sharp juice.

Anna concentrated on stirring her coffee. "Lots of things. I thank God for stuff, tell Him how amazing I find Him and what I'm worried about. I pray for my friends and family and for the CU. Things like that anyway."

"Do you pray for me?" I asked.

"Yes."

I leant forward, interested. "What do you pray?"

Anna carefully thought about her words. I tried to work out why this was difficult for her. Sarah had always tried to be so open, the one pushing the conversation against my defences. Maybe I'd forced her to be...

"I pray that God will bless you. That He would look after you, and... that you would become a Christian."

I put down my apple. "Really? Why? What if I don't need religion?"

Anna took a deep, determined breath and looked me in the face. Her words came out in a rush. "Everyone needs God, Izzy. Being a Christian isn't about a psychological crutch, to help us cope with life, or an intellectual game. We need Him desperately or we're in massive trouble."

I leant back in my seat, taken aback by her sudden forwardness. "What is it about then?" I asked quietly. My question was genuine. I wished I'd asked Sarah and finally understood her.

Anna paused to think. "It's like if you had a horrible bacterial infection and I had the antibiotics to treat it. You don't believe you're ill so don't take the treatment I give you. You're going to die if you don't take them whether you believe you're sick or not. It's the same with God. If He's true and says we're in trouble unless we accept His help, then it makes no difference whether you believe in Him or not. You're still in trouble. Deciding whether God is true is the biggest decision you will ever make because it will affect you for all eternity."

"Not if he doesn't exist it won't," I said, slightly taken aback by this more passionate Anna. "Then whatever religion you follow doesn't affect you after you die. There's no eternity. You just die."

"That has to be the assumption you make beforehand to say the statement 'religion is just for some people'. For that to be true, God has to not exist and just be a fantasy some people cling to. Do you know that for sure? Will you stake your life on it? Your death on it?" She paused. I didn't know how to reply to that. It was true I couldn't say I'd looked into this enough to have as much confidence as Anna as to whether God was true or not. I could see why she thought the decision was so important. I'd never thought about it like that before.

Anna pulled a Bible from her bag. "I'm normally rubbish at

explaining or showing anyone Christian stuff, I know so little, but we did the answer to that very question in CU Central three days ago." Anna was slightly shaking her head in amazement. "Why does everyone need God? What is humanity's biggest problem? We did this passage." She opened a pretty purple Bible in front of me and read a passage she said was from 'Luke'. It was about a band of friends who carry a paralysed friend to see Jesus and when they can't reach him due to the crowd, they lower him from the ceiling. She held it in front of both of us so I could follow the text.

"What are these friends expecting Jesus to do?" asked Anna, excitedly, pausing the story.

I was caught off guard being asked a question about a text I knew nothing about. I'd never read the Bible. "Er… heal him I suppose, so he can walk. Since it said at the beginning he's famous for these miracles."

Anna smiled. "Exactly. But what does he do first? Here, this is the next sentence."

I paused, and then read the next sentence aloud. *"When Jesus saw their faith, he said, 'Friend, your sins are forgiven.'"* I looked up at her questioningly. My mind was blank as to how these things fitted together. I would have been annoyed if Jesus had said that to me instead of healing my legs.

Anna, however, pointed to the verse as if she was amazed it was there. "Exactly. Our sins are what we have done wrong in our life. When we have hurt others, especially God. That includes ignoring Him who loves us and made us, who deserves our loyalty more than anyone else." She pointed at the verse again and paused for me to think, but was bursting with nerves and excitement at the same time. "Isn't that crazy? Look at Jesus' priorities. It was more important for that man's sins to be forgiven than for him to be able to walk! Being sinful is worse than being paralysed! Even in that society! Jesus dealt with his biggest need first, his biggest problem!" She turned back to the text and showed the next verses with her finger. "Then the Jewish teachers are upset because only God can forgive sins so Jesus is claiming to be God. Therefore they accuse him of blasphemy. So then Jesus heals the paralysed man physically *just to prove* that the man has indeed been healed of his *sins* as that is so much more important!"

I paused to think, to try to work out what on Earth Anna was so excited about. I picked up my apple again and traced the smooth skin with my fingers.

"So is it saying the man was paralysed because he was so sinful?" I ventured.

"No, no, no! We're all like him, all sinful and messed up. We were created good and perfect but then fell away from that. We want to go our own way and not God's. We hurt other people and ourselves but most of all we hurt God. This event applies to everybody."

I thought about what she was saying and why she was saying it to me, then sat back and folded my arms, defensive. "So you're saying my biggest problem is my sin?"

"Yes."

"And the situation I'm in now is worse than being paralysed in the first century?"

Anna nodded excitedly. "Yes and only God can forgive you as He's the one who we have rebelled against. That is why you can't say God is only for some people. Without Him you're in a bad way."

I frowned slightly, looking for what was being said between the lines. "You mean I'm going to Hell?"

Anna's excitement turned sober. "If you don't ask for forgiveness then you will receive the punishment that you, that we all, deserve. God won't sweep evil under the carpet, He will see it dealt with and justice served."

I snorted. "Doesn't sound like a very loving God to me."

"Think about that statement, Izzy. He's loving enough to have *died* for you, to pay for what you have done, so you could have complete, free forgiveness, yet justice still prevails. Think what suffering He went through! He's loving enough to forgive anyone who asks sincerely. We don't have to pay Him back or earn His forgiveness. That's why the Bible is such good news."

Her eyes locked with mine, so intense. It was the first time I'd seen her like this. The conversation was so weird, so fanatical. It was strange that she believed this. Didn't she have the same hundreds of questions going around her head as I did? How could she settle on a single ideology? I felt awkward and didn't know what she expected of me so I changed the topic.

*

On Friday nights, Chloe, Mike and I started a tradition of going clubbing together with the floor below. I had an hour of netball then would come back to shower, relax for an hour, eat dinner and then Chloe and I would do our make-up together. She'd recently got a tray of different fake jewels to stick on your skin and was currently putting a diamond one in the corner of each of my eyes. She was wearing a tiny crop top, no bra, and a tight skirt and had massive heels waiting by the door. I'd gone for a simple white dress with the most enhancing bra I had to try to impress Mike and keep his eyes on me all night. I did feel slightly jealous that he would be able to see so much female skin all around him, pushed up against him. I hoped he wouldn't enjoy it too much. It made me feel like I had to compete.

"You sure you're going to be able to handle your drink this time?" I teased Chloe with a smile. Last week I'd spent most of the night holding her hair back as she vomited and making her drink water. In the morning it had been a disgusting clean-up which I had done with Anna. I'd been amazed she hadn't complained or even mentioned to Chloe that she'd helped clean up her mess.

She grinned. "Hold still, Izzy or you'll end up with this in your eye!" The glue finally set and she removed the tweezers from my face, leaning back to check everything was symmetrical. "I'm going to be just sober enough to make sure I don't end up here tonight."

"You mean it's over between you and John?" I asked. I always struggled to keep up with Chloe's romances but I could remember John because she'd actually brought him to the flat so I'd met him.

Chloe shrugged. "Yeah. That was always an open relationship anyway."

I paused in thought. "Chloe, does it ever bother you that some people think what you're doing is wrong?" I suddenly realised how offensive my words sounded and wished I could take them back.

Chloe stopped bending down to turn off her hair curlers. The smell of burnt dust was slowly filling the room. "What you saying?" She frowned at me and I tensed.

"Sorry, I meant, well I was thinking this morning how everyone has their different opinions on what is all right to do with men and relationships and stuff, and people often feel so strongly and judge each other. One of the team didn't turn up to netball today and everyone was really bitchy about her, saying how she'd slept with half her Hall and the other half are mostly female, you know. They were all so against her yet they must have different boundaries and views themselves... I just don't get it. How can they suddenly turn on somebody like that when they can't define what's right and wrong themselves? Or give much logical reason behind their own boundaries?"

Chloe looked at me strangely then bent over to turn off her curling iron. "What's got you asking, Izzy? If you're worried I'll get hurt by bitchy comments, it's fine, I don't care. What I'm doing isn't hurting anyone so why is it anyone's business?"

I nodded. *'Do what you like as long as it doesn't hurt anyone.'* It seemed to be what everyone said when I tried to push them. "So have you never got hurt?" I asked, picking up the hair spray to give my curls an extra layer.

"Course I have. Everyone gets their heart broken and breaks hearts, that's what growing up is about." She paused and looked at me sideways past her glossy dark curls. "Is something going on between you and Mike? Something you're not comfortable with."

I shook my head and smiled. "Sorry, Chloe, I'm just being silly. I keep over thinking things ever since... well ever since I left school." *When Sarah died.* Why couldn't I ever tell people about her? It was like her death would have less of a hold on me if nobody knew.

Chloe smiled and started to pack her clutch. "No worries. Relationships are hard. You realise Mike will break your heart too? You need to toughen yourself for it, don't let yourself get too dependent or it will hurt more. That's why I find it easier to be with guys for a short time. I miss them less. Stops me feeling too much. Helps me keep my independence. It's just physical pleasure."

I paused. "What do you mean Mike will break my heart?"

Chloe laughed at me. "You're so naive. Well you're not planning on marrying him are you? You're just dating him for

94

fun. Do you even love him? Well one day it's going to end. Remember that when you daydream. What you're doing is the same as me, using relationships for pleasure now. I'm just doing it with more boys. You just don't hurt anyone."

I frowned, not liking the way she'd put that. I wasn't like Chloe was I? "What about me? How do I not get hurt myself?" How did you make sure nobody got hurt?

Chloe laughed. "Don't date!" She pulled out a bottle of vodka and one of Coke from under her bed and poured two large shots. "Come on, Izzy, stop your worrying. Right now life is good. Let's drink ready for tonight."

Chapter Eight

I was lying on Mike's bed texting old school friends and flicking through their Facebook pictures. They all seemed to be having so much fun at Uni. Nothing but wave after wave of smiling faces and positive captions. It was like I was the only one with a care in the world. I had my feet over Mike's lap, wiggling my toes to help the nail varnish to dry, while he played Xbox. A shout from Anna made me jump. She was knocking on the doors one by one calling us to the sitting room. I took one last look at Mike's bare back, running my big toe down it before he reached to grab a T-shirt. I liked his back and the way the muscles moved over his shoulder blades. Tom from school had had the best back.

Mike saved his game and stretched. He leant over and kissed my tummy before helping me up by dragging me off the bed by my wrists. He hugged me from behind and marched me out of the room while I laughed, my legs being propelled by his. Life did feel so much better when I was with him. Perhaps I was falling in love.

He marched me into the kitchen where Anna was arranging loads of coloured card, tinsel and glue on the table. "You have to be kidding me," muttered Mike into my hair.

Anna clapped her hands for attention. "They've announced the competition for best decorated flat. It just needs to be in the communal areas. And the winners get half price tickets for the 'Snow Ball'. Guys we can sooo do this."

Holly was lounged over the sofa in trackies and bare feet. She was already sticking cotton wool onto a cut out of a snowman. "Sounds like a scam from the cleaners to make us clean the kitchen, but if I'm allowed to use glitter, I'm game," she grinned. It was so nice to see her doing something other than work or exercise. Her computer was loading a Spotify Christmas playlist beside her.

I'd always loved decorating the house for Christmas and the idea of doing it here, all together, suddenly made the flat more like a real home. I sat down and grabbed some of the card. "I'll make some paper chains. Anna can't you make those pompom tissue paper things?"

She grinned. "Already made a load."

Mike rubbed a hand through his hair. "Well it looks like you're all sorted without me." He started to walk back to his Xbox.

Anna grabbed his hand from behind and shoved a load of glittering tinsel at him. "Na ah. You're the only one who can reach the ceiling to put some of these things up. Chloe can instruct where."

Mike sighed. "This is what I get for being the only boy! Fred wouldn't have put up with this…"

"Oh stop your complaining, hun," I said. "You'll love it," I grinned at him.

By the time I was about three meters into my paper chain we were all hyper from glitter, sweets and fizzy drinks. A Christmas playlist was on full blast and we joined in periodically. Holly was making an ambitious 3D Santa to sit outside the flat door. Mike was on his computer editing pictures of us to go on our doors wearing Santa hats and with elves at our feet. He was amusing himself by finding the worst pictures he could on Facebook. Chloe was not impressed and kept on demanding a better photo of herself. There were so many drunken or revealing pictures of her that Mike was just winding her up again and again and I had to break in to stop her from getting upset.

Chloe's ring tone went off. She sighed and mouthed that it was her mum. Chloe's mum always seemed to talk for hours to her. She answered the phone and left the flat, going to the lobby where there was a better signal and no music.

Anna watched her go and then checked down the corridor. "She's left her room unlocked," she hissed excitedly. "Let's prank it!"

We desperately exchanged ideas trying to decide what to do as quickly as possible. There was the one where you turned everything upside down; or the one where you wrapped everything in clingfilm. The one where you filled the floor with full cups of water, stole the bed, or filled it with balloons.

"Why don't we cover everything with clingfilm and then stick glitter to it? She won't notice the clingfilm and will panic. Plus she'll be finding glitter in her bed and hair for weeks!" suggested Anna.

We looked at each other and nodded, then ran giggling into Chloe's room. Mike rolled his eyes and continued finding silly photos of us on Facebook without Chloe to argue against them.

Holly brought all the clingfilm we had in the house and she and Anna started to wrap text books up in it while I covered the bed. Soon there was glitter everywhere, on my hands, in my hair, ingrained in the carpet. Holly had been trying to glitter her clingfilmed laptop and then managed to spill the whole tube onto the keyboard. We all paused and hoped the clingfilm would be enough protection to stop it jamming the keys. Anna was taking photos on her phone.

I hadn't seen Holly ever seem this happy and I realised I'd misjudged her. She'd always seemed so boring, always working, always stressed and never coming out. Then she spent so many of her weekends away with her boyfriend from school. But I guessed this was who she really was. I thought we really needed to do things together as a flat more. Anna had been trying to initiate more cinema trips and things, but I'd been so caught up in time with Mike I'd barely ever taken her offers up. I needed to change that before I turned into one of those people who ditched her friends as soon as she got a boyfriend.

Anna suddenly hissed for us to be quiet. Footsteps up to the front door! We ran back into the kitchen and pretended to still be cutting things out. Chloe walked back into the flat and came straight into the kitchen. She tossed her phone onto the work surfaces and bounced herself down onto the sofa. Then she realised we were all being far too quiet and stifling giggles.

"What's wrong with you people?" She paused, eyeing up each of us in turn. Anna cracked and started to laugh. "What have you done?"

She got up and disappeared down the corridor as she walked to her room. We all listened for a scream of shock or laughter. There were a few minutes of silence and I suddenly worried she would fail to see the funny side. Nobody normally messed with Chloe; she was always so sure of herself and quick to bite back. The silence continued. *Quick to bite back...*

"Oh no," I gasped. Everyone turned to me. "I've left my door open!"

I ran back to my room. Chloe had just finished wedging my

mattress out of the window so that the only thing stopping it falling two storeys was the half closed window holding the corner. If I tried to free it, it would be difficult to not let it fall. Chloe slapped her hands together and put her hands in her pockets.

"What the…" I smiled back at her. "You can't blame it all on me, you know."

"I don't intend to," she grinned and brought out a tube of glitter from each pocket. Then she sauntered back to the kitchen, leaving me to struggle with the mattress. I would definitely need Mike to hold its weight while I opened the window. I wedged it a bit more securely and was about to call for help. Then the screams in the kitchen started and shrieks and thuds as people ran about. I grinned and decided I'd wait for things to die down.

*

The Christmas holidays came around so fast I couldn't believe it especially since the second years all said your first term at Uni definitely felt the longest. I was already having to revise for our first exams, and was finding the prospect stressful even though they didn't count overall. They were so much harder to predict than A levels and so many of the marks seemed to depend on the preferred essay style of the person who happened to mark it. Three years was suddenly a very short time. I was looking forward to seeing Mum again but when I finally got home I found it really strange. In the last few months I'd got used to spending my time however I wished, with whomever I wished. I'd got used to deciding when to get up and go to bed. I'd got used to constant company and noise and fun.

Suddenly the house was eerily quiet and if I was feeling bored or lonely, there was no instant release of friends everywhere. I suddenly didn't have an activity every single evening. And Mum saw me as exactly the same girl I was three months ago. She didn't know that I'd changed and was used to a different way of life. I was still just a schoolgirl to her to be scolded when necessary.

I found the contrast so difficult that I sometimes had to go to the bathroom to stop myself from crying. Why was I so emotional? And worse, Sarah was everywhere. In my bedroom, lying in her favourite green jumper on my bed. Brushing her hair with my mirror. Making hot chocolate or tea in the kitchen. She'd been here so much. I hadn't realised what an escape Uni had been. I sat on my bed and pretended she was still there. I remembered when we had first invented our Pride and Prejudice game. We'd both read the book multiple times and watched the T.V. series to death. When we realised we both knew it so well, we would lie down on our backs, one person's legs over the other's and take it in turns to read a sentence out of the book. The other person had to predict the sentence after and would get points on accuracy. Every time we had ended up being silly and introducing ridiculous conversations and plot twists. I hadn't ever been able to share something like that with anyone else. I hadn't even told anyone else about our game, it would sound so boring and nerdy.

Mum asked question after question about Mike followed by warnings about getting pregnant and making sure he was good enough for me. Mike was skiing with his family in France for three weeks so I couldn't see him and I missed him terribly. I texted him every few hours but he was rubbish at replying and I had little to say. At least I could hide myself away in revision instead of trying to dissect my complicated emotions and reactions.

*

When I finally got back to Uni I had the strange sensation of coming home again. This was where I belonged now and where I was most myself. Holly and Anna had already started exams and only had one left so I was the third person to arrive. It was so nice to catch up with them in revision breaks over tea in the kitchen. Then Chloe was back. She was completely caught up in this project she was behind on, that I didn't understand at all. Finally Mike came home, the afternoon before our exam.

As soon as I heard his door open and close I ran out to greet him. I was about to throw myself on him when I awkwardly realised his dad was still in the room, looking smart in a suit. Mike made introductions and I smiled and shook his hand, keenly aware that my blouse was unbuttoned one below what I normally had. His father asked easy, polite questions and then Mike walked back with him to the car, winking at me as he closed the door.

I was left in his room feeling like a lemon. Then I shook myself and stretched out on Mike's bed in a position I thought was probably sexy, my mind buzzing from revision. I felt as prepared as I could for tomorrow's timed essay; I just wanted Mike to unwind me before I went over things one last time.

I must have dozed off because I woke to Mike sitting down beside me on his bed. I noticed he'd got a tan skiing that ended in funny places. He was smiling that cheeky grin he got before he was about to suggest something fun or naughty. He didn't seem stressed by revision at all.

"Hmm, I seem to have somebody in my bed. How did they get there?" He brushed my cheek with a finger and then tugged on a strand of hair.

I smiled. "Maybe they were waiting for you? Maybe they were desperate for you?" I faked a pout.

Then he was kissing me and our clothes were suddenly thrown onto the floor. I dimly hoped he'd remembered to lock the door.

Mike had picked up some new ideas that he'd 'seen' or 'heard of' so it was a lot later than I'd planned when I finally got back to my room. I couldn't shake a feeling of discomfort that he'd probably been watching a lot of porn over the holiday. How on Earth was I supposed to compete with that? It made me feel like I had to pretend to find everything incredibly enjoyable and had to work hard to please him. It felt like I was being compared and my body was just something to be used.

*

The exam was intense but just about all right. As we filed out of the hall I kept on worrying that I'd misread some aspect of the title that meant I'd answered the wrong thing, or left out an important perspective of the argument. I still couldn't get Mike out of my head. I needed to open up more with Chloe for advice. She had lots of experience. I just wasn't sure that she was the sort of person I wanted to be.

My year swept out of the building in a frenzy of comparing answers and revision and how hard it had been. Stories of the holidays were just starting to become appropriate as people wound down. Then it was announced by Harry, wobbling on a chair armrest, that the whole year should go to the Brass Pig for drinks before all going clubbing at Syndicate or Lounge.

There were cheers and laughter and I realised I hadn't heard sounds like that for weeks.

I felt myself be swept along without even consciously making the decision to go. I wasn't wearing any make-up and had comfy exam clothes on, but then everyone was in the same boat. It gave everything a more relaxed feel. I enjoyed the buzz that followed the release of stress as everyone shared stories and jokes.

A few hours later most people were drunk and in Lounge since Syndicate had been deemed too far away and people were already tired and lazy, and some were throwing up. As I was buying a round of drinks a girl in my year I'd never spoken to before ended up next to me in the queue. She was incredibly sober.

"Hi, I'm Laura," she said. "You're Izzy right?" She had light brown wavy hair and the fashion scarf and cardigan, girlie look.

I nodded. "You've clearly got a better memory than me."

She shook her head. "Not at all. I know your flatmate Anna and she's pointed you out before when I said we were on the same course. I've been to your flat twice but you were out."

"Oh, small world, hey? How do you know Anna?" I already knew the answer before she said it. She would be one of those Christians who excitedly greeted her in the streets.

"We go to the same church and have mutual friends back at her home. Hey, we're going to the cinema on Saturday afternoon. Want to join? Mike's welcome too of course. Sophie is also coming." She pointed to another historian who'd once helped me find a book in the library. "She's on my corridor, and I think your flatmate Holly told Anna she'd go so it'll be a nice group."

I'd been starting to feel bad about turning down so many of

Anna's invites. "Yeah, sure." Why not? I needed to get to know people on my course better anyway, especially with everyone suddenly talking about getting accommodation next year and arguments starting about people being left out of group houses. I'd assumed we stay as a flat and rent somewhere more central, but Mike was getting fed up being the only guy and he found Anna a bit too much sometimes.

Laura smiled. "Great, see you then." And then she had her drinks and carried them back to where Sophie was chatting with Harry.

I grabbed my drinks, trying to remember who they were for and pushed my way back into the sweaty crowd. Where was Mike? I didn't think he would want to come to the cinema with another group of girls.

Then I spotted him. He was completely off his face, leaning on one of his mate's shoulders, laughing too loud. I rolled my eyes. Maybe it was time to head home. I delivered the drinks and then navigated up to him. He drunkenly spread his arms out to me.

"Izzy! How's m' beau'iful girl?" One of his hands strayed to my chest and I pushed his arm off in embarrassment.

"Mike! What you doing? Not here!"

He laughed and pulled me into him. "Just joking, babe. Let me make it up to ya." He grinned and tried to kiss me, squished at an angle, his breath rank with drink. I pushed him off, incredibly uncomfortable.

"I think you should go home, Mike," I said and stalked off. One of Mike's friends mimicked being slapped in the face and they laughed.

He's just drunk. Nothing to be upset about. Let's just go home and not let him make an idiot of the both of us.

I drank half of my drink and then pushed it towards

somebody else, looking for a way to escape. Kyla and Jess, the other two Durdhamites in my year were standing by the door with their coats on. I thanked God and hurried over to them to ask to share whatever means of transport they were leaving with.

They smiled tiredly at me and said there was time to catch the last bus back if we hurried. I nodded, checking everything was still in my handbag before leaving.

"Isn't Mike coming?" asked Kyla, trying to hide impatience.

"No, he's..." I turned around to look for him in the crowd. He was dancing with Jayne who I often sat next to in lectures. She was much better endowed than me and I felt threatened. He was so drunk he kept on bumping into her. Then one hand was around her waist, then her bum. I frowned and started to push my way towards them. Then he was kissing her. Properly kissing her. And she was kissing back, her hand tangled in his hair. *Bitch*!

I spun and strode out the door, holding back angry tears. "Mike is clearly otherwise engaged!"

*

I burst back into the flat and went straight to Chloe's room where I started to drip mascara stained tears onto her bed. She was still awake and doing her project on the computer but turned it all off when I entered and snuggled me into her as I told her what happened.

"Oh, Izzy, he's an idiot. But don't worry; it doesn't have to mean all that! He was probably too drunk and she took advantage of him. He might not even remember in the morning. Try not to take it too hard. You can easily avoid Jayne if you want to."

106

"He will remember if he wakes up in her bed tomorrow," I sobbed.

Chloe rolled her eyes. "If he does, dump him. Easy. If it's just a drunken kiss, well, if you're still having a good time together, make him spoil you rotten for a few weeks to earn your forgiveness. You can still be in control, Izz." She held up my chin and looked into my face. "Now go and get some sleep and try not to think about it. The more you think about it, the worse it will seem, when it probably meant nothing at all."

I nodded and smiled weakly. Chloe grabbed her laptop and snapped it open again. "This will distract you. Holly has found us all a flat for next year. Just our flat plus one of Anna and Holly's medic friends, George, that also plays football with Mike, so he won't be the only guy." She flicked through the pictures. "Isn't it nice? And it's so cheap for somewhere that central. Isn't that amazing? And look double beds and two bathrooms instead of one."

I nodded. It did look nice. I had no idea what an acceptable price was for renting a house, but was happy to trust them. "Holly wants us all to go down to sign tomorrow afternoon at the estate agents, so you have all morning to sort it out with Mike."

No pressure! If Holly had found this yesterday, I'd have been so excited. Now I wasn't so sure. If I fell out with Mike, I didn't really want to live with him anymore.

I washed my face in her sink and said I'd try to just think about the flat, before leaving her room. *Probably meant nothing at all*. But seeing him do that had hurt so much. It made me feel like I was being ripped inside, like all our intimacy meant nothing. Part of me, a wild part of me, wanted to find another boy to kiss to show him what it felt like. But I

107

didn't want another boy. I wanted Mike. And anyway, I'd always felt strongly about cheating. I was such a weak idiot! Why couldn't I be as hard and controlled as Chloe? Or did she just want us to stay together so as not to mess up the flat? I shook my head. How could I think something so mean?

I fumbled back into my room and lay down on my bed trying to not think about it. Even as I tried, tears rolled silently out of the corners of my eyes and I had to hold my breath to stop sobs erupting from my chest.

A knock at the door. Only Anna knocked that softly. I didn't reply. Anna knocked again. "Izzy, are you all right?" Silence. "May I come in?"

She slowly pushed the door open and crept quietly in beside me. I didn't move, I didn't want to talk about it again, but she sat down on the bed and moved my head onto her lap and started to stroke my hair. She said nothing, but it felt nice.

After ten minutes the tears had stopped and I just felt empty. "Laura, my friend on your course, told me what happened. I'm so sorry, Izzy."

I sat up and shrugged. "She should mind her own business." I blew my nose on a tissue and smeared mascara across my face with the back of my hand.

Anna paused. "What I wanted to tell you was, if you've seen the house for next year, but don't want to live with Mike, you should say. It's just a house, we can find another one. I didn't want you to feel pressured, that's all. Holly spent a long time finding it so is a bit fixated, but everyone would understand. Holly's split up with her boyfriend this holiday so is a bit emotional, and trying to use up all her free time. She'd find another one no problem."

"Holly didn't tell me that. I suppose I've barely seen her." I sighed. "Thanks, Anna. I don't know what I'm going to do yet.

Chloe thinks I should forgive him if he's willing to make it up to me. Just a drunken kiss and all that."

"What do you feel about him?" Anna asked, leaning forward so she could wrap an arm around me.

"Hurt. Illogically so." The tears were starting again.

"It's not illogical. You were sleeping with Mike so you shared something incredibly intimate and private with him. You've given him so much of you, you want and need him to treasure it, not get distracted by another woman. If he's prone to that when very drunk, he shouldn't get very drunk."

"But if I split up with him, it will hurt even more," I sobbed.

Anna squeezed my arm. "I know, lovely. It's your decision and yours alone. Just don't let the house come into it." She rested her forehead on my hair and then left the room.

I collapsed back down again. I liked Mike so much; I was beginning to wonder if I was falling in love with him. Yet we'd just lasted a single university term. Three measly months. I really wanted Sarah right now. Even though she'd tell me off for getting intimate too quickly and then I would shout at her for being a know-it-all about things she had no experience in and we'd leave cross. I really needed her.

*

I woke up with puffy eyes at 11:30am. I had a shower, got dressed and ate breakfast solemnly. I needed time to prepare myself for what was to come.

I banged on Mike's door and entered before he had time to finish shuffling. The room was dark so I turned on the light. Mike was halfway through getting dressed. Part of me was relieved at the evidence that he had indeed spent the night here. He walked up to me, topless and attempted his cheeky grin.

109

"What did you think you were doing?" I shouted at him, biting my lip to help keep the tears in.

He tried to put a hand on my shoulder but I shrugged it off immediately. "Calm down, Izzy! I'm sorry, all right? I was drunk and stupid. I can barely remember it. It didn't mean anything."

"Didn't it? What does it mean when you kiss *me* then? That you 'love me?'" I shoved him backwards away from me. "You've never told me you do." I shoved him again even though it didn't budge him. "That you're attracted to me? Well surely that's what that kiss last night meant? That you found her attractive?"

"Izzy, I'm sorry all right?" He raised his hands in front of him in defence. "It was wrong. What else am I supposed to say? It's not like I slept with her or anything!"

I was crying now and it was becoming hard to breathe properly. I wanted to scream at him and hit him but I didn't even know what I wanted from him. I didn't even know if I was being unreasonable. I turned and ran.

Once in my room I attempted to slam the anti-slamming door and picked up my phone and took deep breaths to control my voice through the tears. I flicked down to Mum but then paused. I knew what she would say. She would say that it was all Mike's fault; it was just unlucky I had dated a loser. Men are often like that; don't let your expectations of relationships get too high. After all I'd never loved him, had I? I had just wanted to have fun. So now I needed to have some fun elsewhere. She would make me feel better by telling me how wonderful I was and that Mike was an idiot not to see it. For some reason that wasn't what I wanted to hear right now. It's how most girls dealt with breakups, trying to make themselves feel better and at the same time slagging off the men, but it lacked any substance. I didn't want to be treated like this by men and see this as normal. I wanted to speak to Sarah and hear her fairy tale like vision of relationships, even if I knew that was naive and impossible.

My thumb scrolled up with a will of its own. Sarah's mum. I hadn't realised I still had her number. Would she find it weird if I rang her? Especially for relationship advice. Her marriage always appeared so healthy. I wanted to be like her, not my mum with no self-esteem and a series of broken relationships. I imagined Merilyn at home right now, perhaps cleaning. No children to pass her wisdom to anymore. If Sarah was still alive they would have had long conversations about Uni every week. Sarah had always talked to her mum about everything. Well now that she was gone, maybe... well maybe she could advise me instead.

I pushed the call button before I could over think it any more. It rang for ages and I almost hung up before Sarah's mum picked it up with a hurried 'hello'.

I licked my lips in nervousness. What I was doing was crazy. "Mrs Holland? Merilyn?"

"Speaking?"

"It's Izzy. Izzy Maids."

There was a pause down the phone. "Izzy! Goodness, but it's good to hear your voice again. I'm so glad you've decided to ring. How are you? How's Bristol?"

She'd even remembered what University I was going to. "I... I..." To my shame I started to cry again.

"Oh, Izzy, whatever is the matter, dear? Would you like me to ring back?"

"No... I... Do you think it's possible to have a completely happy relationship?" I blurted out in a rush.

"Oh, Izzy. I'm sorry to say that no, I don't think any

relationship that involves us humans can be perfect, because we are selfish and broken. We inflict that on each other. In this life, anyway."

"Then why get married?" I asked. I wanted to hear about her own life and not let her know what I'd done as I knew she would disapprove of sex outside of marriage. She'd think I had got what I deserved.

"Just because something isn't perfect, dear, and is hard work doesn't mean that it's not very, very good and absolutely worth fighting for. Relationships, whether friends, family or husbands are all crucial to our lives. Your relationship with Sarah often wasn't easy but it was so precious to her." She paused as if debating whether to continue. "Do you know what the Bible says one of the main purposes of marriage is? Why we long for a perfect relationship?"

"No," I replied, mildly uncomfortable but eager for her to keep talking in her calm voice, eager to understand. I wanted to learn what was behind all these confusing words and concepts.

"Marriage now is a foretaste of the perfect relationship we were created to have, to long for. The one we're meant to have with God." She paused for it to sink in. "One day the Bible says the Church, as in all Christians, will be married to Jesus in a perfect relationship. That day is when He returns to Earth and makes the world perfect." She paused again. "Our marriages now are imperfect 'adverts' to how incredible our marriage with Christ will be for eternity. That's why we all long for that *perfect* relationship. We're built for it, Izzy. The world makes films and stories about it. But you can't find it on Earth. It only exists with Christ. That's why we feel so let down when relationships aren't perfect on Earth. Even though we know they won't be. It still hurts. They're meant to make us long for something more."

My brain felt sluggish processing her argument that felt so strange. The things I'd heard about the 'End of the World' according to Christianity hadn't sounded like that. "But Sarah said we can have good relationships on Earth."

"Yes, because God gives us good gifts now. He can bless us extravagantly. I'm very happy in my marriage but that doesn't come easily. It's helpful to remember that the good in it is just a pale reflection of what the future will hold because it is just an advert," she repeated. "Of a perfect relationship with Jesus. I love that it keeps me looking forward to the future. It makes me remember all my wants and desires don't need to be fulfilled right now in my husband. It takes that impossible burden off him and stops us from crushing each other. Instead we can give each other space and help each other grow into better, more loving people."

I chewed my lip feeling very confused and just wanting to hear the practical advice, not the theology. "So what do you think makes a good relationship?"

"Lots of things, my dear, like being truthful, open, good communication, selflessness, praying together, but none of those are the most important. That is having Jesus at the centre of your marriage."

"What does that mean?" I said, trying to not get frustrated.

"It means sharing your faith with each other and so putting what God wants first. For example, with your money, time and house; He leads you in countercultural ways. It means that as a couple you love and treasure each other no matter what because Jesus has loved and forgiven us. Even if one of us does something really bad, the other can remember how Jesus forgave them and so feel able to forgive in return. The Bible says a man should love his wife as Christ loved the Church. That means being willing to give up everything for her, even his own life! It means he loves and values her unconditionally. He should put her above himself every single day, every single moment. And in return the wife respects and submits to her husband. In our culture, it is so common for wives to complain and gossip about their husbands behind their backs, or try to make it out as if they're always in the wrong. They collude that men are always the unreasonable ones. Instead the Bible says we need to learn to truly value them, not try to gain superiority, but always talk about them respectfully and lovingly as they should you. It involves praying and supporting each other. It's beautiful."

"But, Merilyn, I don't believe in God."

Sarah's mum paused again. "Why not?"

Her question completely took me aback. That was the question Christians were meant to get, 'Why believe?' Disbelief was the default. I hadn't expected to ever be asked the reverse.

"Because... because it doesn't make sense. There's not enough evidence."

"Have you ever looked for evidence, Izzy?" came Merilyn's gentle voice.

I felt myself blush. "Eh, no, not really." Somehow I didn't think Descartes and Thomas Aquinas were what she was referring to.

"Why not?"

"Because... because I've never needed religion. It's just not my thing." Anna's voice came back to me. *Everyone needs God.*

"Izzy, choosing whether to follow God or not is the biggest decision you will ever make. It will affect every other decision you make in this life and how you see death. Are you going to gamble your eternal happiness or grief on the assumption that there is no afterlife? When you've not even looked at the evidence? It doesn't matter whether you're religious or not. If you're *not* following Jesus, you'd better make completely sure God doesn't exist. He either does or He doesn't. There's no neutral ground in this."

I thought her argument through and had to admit she was right. University was a time for thinking through different beliefs and lifestyles. I shouldn't just assume anything without checking first. My lecturers always told me to search for the original accounts of events and not just accept one historian's viewpoint with no evidence. One set of events happened. The truth of how the events were presented might be relative and people might see different truths, but fundamentally something either happened or it didn't, whatever the postmodernist says. So many of our lecturers were postmodernists, saying truth is individual to a person, according to their perspective. It sounded deep and clever but sometimes it was crucial to know what had actually happened. Like did the Nazis really perform the Holocaust? The truth behind that was too big and important to say it was just defined by people's perceptions. Whether Jesus really did live and rise from the dead was the same.

"How do I look for the evidence?"

"God gave us two massive pieces of evidence. One is the Bible. A collection of books and letters written by multiple authors over thousands of years that say the same story over and over again and talk about the same God. The other is the strongest piece of evidence you can imagine."

"What, stronger than God appearing in my bedroom, with a massive sign saying 'I exist?'"

Merilyn chuckled. "Very close. But not just appearing to you but to thousands of people for thirty-three years, teaching and proving Himself with miracles. He went around saying look at me, I exist, follow me. And then, after we killed Him in disbelief because we refused to believe the evidence right before our faces, He rose from the dead. We then have eyewitness accounts of Him being seen by individuals and whole crowds. That's a lot of evidence, dear."

"But that was two thousand years ago."

"Yes and we have more documentation and eyewitness accounts of Jesus than of Julius Caesar. But beware, Izzy. People who were *there* two thousand years ago, who saw Him raise people from the dead, and saw people die rather than deny they'd seen *Jesus* raised from the dead, still denied Him. The evidence was staring them in the face, but it was the matter of their hearts. They didn't *want* to believe despite the overwhelming evidence. Becoming a Christian was too inconvenient. They were too proud."

I shuffled on my bed uncomfortably. I didn't want it to be true either. I didn't want to completely change the way I lived my life or have to go to church or be seen as weird by my course mates.

"Izzy, let me respectfully give you a challenge. One that Sarah herself did years ago. Find out the truth for yourself. Don't let fear of it being true stop you looking for evidence. And if you find enough evidence to be convincing, be convinced from an unbiased standpoint. Don't deny it just because it will affect your life. If you don't find enough evidence, then you know you can reject it. You can do the same for the other religions and ideologies. Read books. Use the internet. Get Christians at Uni to read the Bible with you."

I paused and felt determination rise. I could prove this wrong, I knew I could. How could there possibly be enough convincing evidence when basically nobody believed it anymore? I thought back to the start of the conversation. "So how will this help me with my relationships?"

"Izzy, His cross changes everything. You'll see."

I froze at the words that were written in the front cover of Sarah's diary. Words I'd been ignoring. "Merilyn, what does that actually mean?"

I could almost see her smile down the phone. "Oh, Izzy, it would take me hours to say all the ways His cross has changed different areas of my life. At its simplest, I suppose, if you believe that somebody has died in your place, even after seriously offending them, that changes things. Especially if they did it out of love, because they want a relationship with you. It changes how you see yourself. It ties you to them." She paused, thoughtfully. "But His cross is more than that. Because of the cross, God can change us into different people, better people. It affects how you see the world. It changes how you treat others and what you long for in the future. I think, Izzy, there is so much about the cross, you'll need to work out things in your own time."

"Thanks, Merilyn. I'll call you to let you know how I get on."

*

Enough was enough; it was time to pull myself together. I had a plan. No more wallowing in self-pity. I was going to sort out the confused mess of my brain once and for all, and I was going to do it properly. First, I was going to put my relationship on hold with Mike until I could decide what I wanted from it and what I could find acceptable in a boyfriend. If he couldn't wait for me to be ready, then he obviously didn't care about me enough and he could go off and bed Jayne. The more I thought

117

about it, the less likely it felt that he would wait for me. I'd always been temporary. Well this was the test. If I meant nothing to him apart from being attractive, I didn't want to be with him.

Second, I was going to say no to the flat. I didn't want to live with Mike again until I was prepared to move in with him as a long term partner. It would make this all too confusing and emotional. I would have to not be fussy with where I ended up, but I could be strong in this. Live with course mates if I had to.

Third, I was going to explore Christianity. I was going to do it both by myself, to remove the bias of only hearing things from a Christian point of view, but also using Anna's help. I was going to use this time to decide where I stood on issues of morality and why. Hopefully this would help me decide how I wanted to live the rest of my life.

Fourth, I was going to stick those pictures of Sarah back on my wall and meet her every day with a clear conscience, knowing I could justify my actions.

An hour in and my plan was already much harder than I expected.

To "bring the Sword."

Chapter Nine

"What do you mean, you don't want to live with us next year?" shouted Holly. She already had her coat on to head off to the estate agents. I stood in the middle of the kitchen surrounded by the girls.

"Izzy, just because Mike kissed somebody, doesn't mean you have to punish yourself," said Chloe with exaggerated calmness. "You told him you were having a break to work out what you wanted from your relationship, right? Well you could be back with him in a few weeks. If you split up, you could still be friends. Don't you think you're being a bit over dramatic? We're your closest friends here. You can't just break up our house over a fall out that will likely only last a few weeks."

I shuffled my feet. "I'm sorry, guys. It's nothing against you. I just don't want the pressure of living with Mike anymore."

"But I spent ages looking for this house, Izzy, and you've not contributed anything. George, Mike's friend, signed yesterday." Holly flung her hands out and tried to calm herself down. "What do you suggest we do?" she said with heavy annoyance.

"It's just one person difference. There must be lots of people still looking. I shouldn't be too difficult to replace." I couldn't meet their eyes.

"But we want to live with *you*!" said Chloe. "You're feeling over emotional and it's stopping you thinking straight."

"You're just being selfish," said Holly. "It's all sorted! It's a big enough house, just ignore Mike if you want to, don't drag all of us into your ridiculous drama. I didn't inflict my break up on you and we'd been together for two and a half years!"

"It's all right," said Mike appearing at the door, looking a touch dishevelled but not as much as I would've liked. "I'll be the one who drops out. I've talked to George and we're going into one of the football houses. I'm sure you guys will miss me less than Izzy. The estate agent said his signature hasn't secured the house unless you guys sign today. It will be up for grabs again tomorrow."

Holly pulled at her fringe. "But that leaves two spaces to fill! Two out of six and this house is going to be gone by tomorrow. We're going to lose it and you guys have no idea how perfect it is. How much work I've put into it."

Anna put an arm on Holly's shoulder. "We know you've done a lot for us, Holly, but we can sort this out. It's still early, plenty of time. We can find another place, *together*."

Holly shrugged off her arm and stormed back into her room. Anna sighed. Chloe was not looking amused. "I'm sorry," I tried.

"Well, we have a few options," said Anna with enforced brightness. "Some of my Hall CU friends are looking for two people for their flat and they've invited me, but that would always leave people out. It could be a last back-up if everyone else gets spaces and two are left?"

"I can text my friends," mumbled Chloe, "and see if I can

find two people who are willing to sign today." She pushed her hair out of her face, and left, clearly in a mood.

"Is Holly even going to want to live with me after this?" I asked, feeling awful. I turned to Anna. "Maybe you and Holly should go into that house and Chloe and I will find our own accommodation."

Anna gave me a hug. "We'll sort this out together. Don't worry, as soon as we have houses, people will forget this ever happened. My friend's house has two historians in it, Laura and Sophie, so it may be a back-up for you if we really struggle. The other three are from Hall CU. All girls."

I volunteered to make dinner after looking for houses of all different sizes and feeling utterly ignorant as to how to tell if they were good ones. I could see that Holly could easily have spent hours doing this and apparently she'd looked around three with Anna before we'd come back from holiday. I made fajitas and hated the atmosphere as people came to sit up at the table. Nobody knew where Mike had gone. I'd been hoping he'd get me flowers or chocolates to apologise, or do some epic, surprise romantic gesture to win me back, but he'd not spoken to me since I'd asked to put our relationship on hold. I could tell he thought I was being over dramatic. I felt like a pariah. My boyfriend was avoiding me and my friends were all cross with me. Maybe I should just find a house by myself.

Chloe had found an engineering house missing just one person. She only had to mention it for Holly to storm away from the table without her dinner. Chloe spread her hands out in an innocent posture. "I didn't say I was going for it."

"She's just conscious we all have more friends in other areas compared to her," mumbled Anna. "She's worried she'll be left out to fend for herself with people she doesn't know."

Chloe shrugged. "Should have spent more time integrating then instead of visiting her boyfriend."

"I found a house for four," I ventured. "It's on St Michael's Hill, so really central. Big rooms. £380 a month..."

"Too expensive," interrupted Chloe.

We sat in silence for a while and I felt like apologising again but knew it wouldn't help. I felt so alone all over again.

"Guys, we have ages to find a house for four. There's always a second wave in a month or so," said Anna, trying to keep the peace. "No need for us to panic too much now."

We nodded in agreement but the mood in the flat remained sour.

*

I decided to still go to the cinema on Saturday with Anna, Holly, Laura and Sophie. By then the mood in the flat was more stale than sour. It turned out Josh and Fran, Anna's Hall CU leaders were coming too.

On the walk across the Downs to Anna's favourite cinema, the little cosy Orpheus, Laura made a special effort to talk to me. It was so obvious; I guessed Anna had told her what was going on in the flat. Holly avoided me and was talking just to Anna who was also trying to involve Sophie. It was weird being in a group where only three of us weren't Christians. I found myself illogically careful with what I said, hoping I didn't swear by accident or say anything they'd find crude or offensive. How did they live having to watch themselves like that?

After fifteen minutes discussing course matters with Laura, I nodded to where Fran and Josh were talking in the front. After a bit Fran went to talk to Sophie, like a mother who realised her child was being left out. I wondered if they even knew each other. "Are Fran and Josh together?" I asked.

Laura shook her head. "Fran is dating the CU president, Peter, a third year. Rumour is they might get engaged soon. Josh is single."

"Engaged? Isn't she, like, our age?" I asked in shock. I couldn't even imagine thinking about that stuff now.

"They both took gap years, where they met in Zambia. She's twenty, he's twenty-one. It's nice seeing that level of commitment, don't you think?" she asked, swinging the situation on its head. "My parents were married at their age. I find that the weirdest thing."

"Yeah," I agreed.

"Did your parents get married much older?" she asked.

"Mum never married," I said awkwardly.

Laura blushed which made it worse. "Sorry, I didn't mean to just assume…"

I cut her off with a smile and a wave. "No worries, seriously. I'm completely fine with the fact they weren't married."

"Do they still live together?" asked Laura.

I shook my head. "Dad moved to America when Mum was pregnant with Jack, so, fifteen years ago." I hadn't spoken to him since and didn't intend to. I liked to pretend I wasn't related to a man like that. Mum threw all his postcards in the bin and said he would be a bad influence on us.

We collected our tickets and I tried, awkwardly, to find out who I owed the money to. I held back as we filed in so I didn't end up sitting next to Holly. I found myself on the end next to Josh. He smiled that same warm, yet slightly awkward smile at me that he'd given on my first day of Uni. I wondered if Anna had told him about me and Mike and the flat. I hoped she hadn't, I didn't want to feel like a soap opera, with everyone waiting to hear the next episode. He offered me some popcorn and I took a handful.

"How's running the Hall CU?" I asked, failing to think of anywhere else to start. "Anna seems to really enjoy it."

"Good, I'm glad." He shook his fluffy blond fringe from his eyes as an advert for Coke flashed in front of us. "It's getting easier. I found it really hard being in Halls without my second year friends to start with, but now I feel like I'm getting to know your year almost as well. It was a really hard decision to live in, but it's been worth it."

"Anyone converted yet?" I joked.

"Well, yes actually. One guy started to come to church and CU a month ago and has just started to say he believes it for himself. He can't stop telling everyone." Josh smiled to himself.

"Really?" I hadn't been expecting that, especially a boy. "What made him change his mind?"

Josh looked sideways at me. "God did."

I rolled my eyes. "But how?"

"Well he searched and checked out the things the Bible said to be true. He saw for himself the truth and then fell in love with Jesus."

"Oh." It was more logical than I was expecting. I became more serious as I remembered Merilyn's conversation. "It just sounds hard to find the place to start. People keep on telling me to investigate as if it's really easy."

"Well you could let the CU help. The whole Uni CU is putting on a week of events, the first week of March. There are lunch time talks with free lunch, and evening events with free dinner and music. You're also always welcome to Hall CU and church. Anna can take you."

"But don't you guys discuss things about the Bible? I don't know anything; I'd be completely out of place."

Josh winked. "There's more of a range than you would think. Everyone would be happy to have you there and you wouldn't be the only non-Christian."

I changed the conversation to music so as not to commit to anything without meaning to until I was ready. We found we liked a lot of the same bands and then films and I finally felt myself relax after a stressful, horrid week.

After the film Josh handed me a book. "It happens to be the one I've got on me. If you want another, just let me know, I've got others that might be more to your taste, but he's one of my favourite authors. Keep it as long as you like." It was by C.S. Lewis. I'd no idea he'd written anything other than 'The Lion the Witch and the Wardrobe', and its sequels. It was a double volume. The first half was called 'Surprised by Joy'; the second half was called 'Mere Christianity'.

*

Over the next two weeks I let myself become engrossed in my own private project of reading around Christianity and avoiding the rest of my flat, especially Mike. I skipped a few lectures as I was worried about what people would think about me and Mike, and scared of facing Jayne.

I read 'Surprised by Joy' first and loved the historical element to it. It was C.S. Lewis telling the tale of his conversion. It seemed largely intellectual before it became more heartfelt which surprised me. He was clearly quite an intelligent man and the thought of him trying to find meaning and satisfaction in all those different areas of his life before landing on Christianity, as the only thing that had brought him fulfilment, was an interesting concept. He'd explored so many different avenues, including the occult. Surely different people would find meaning in different things, though? Could he really argue that nobody will find true satisfaction in anything but the Christian God? Did everyone really have an inbuilt desire for him? Everyone? You could never prove that scientifically.

'Mere Christianity' was the first apologetics book I had ever read. However, though I thought some arguments were good or clever, they didn't seem to stick or resonate with me. My response to many was, 'so what?' Then I read the atheist 'God Delusion' which had been sitting on my shelf for a couple of years to try to balance it, but found the tone too mocking in places. It was like going back to religious studies at school, to straw man arguments that people had come up with because they were easy to break down. I felt like I wasn't really learning anything. Next I read a short summary of arguments by the famous atheist David Hume, who impressed me more than Dawkins, and was far clearer. By then I was fed up with arguments, and though I felt much more knowledgeable on the subject, none of the arguments were 100% certain. I didn't know how any of this was helping me personally see Jesus as relevant for my life. I'd hoped that after reading these I would *get* Jesus. I'd hoped I would understand what it was all about and then either be able to accept or reject. But I didn't. If God was real, why didn't he just show himself to me? Overwhelm me with strong emotions or speak to me as I was reading these books?

Chloe declared that I'd become really boring and obsessed. She tried to reason with me that a semi breakup with Mike shouldn't shake my life like this. I needed to rely on myself more and realise I was strong and independent, and I didn't need boys to affirm this. I'd not been out clubbing with her for fourteen days, but didn't miss it at all. I was starting to realise I'd often just gone to seem cool, and fun and to be somebody worth knowing. I now saw all the lust and unhealthy drunkenness and meaningless kisses and broken hearts and irresponsible friendships and low self-esteem with people like Jayne kissing people like Mike. It suddenly just felt out of control.

Then Chloe said she'd found me and her a house, and Anna and Holly could go live with her CU friends. It was a mixture of her clubbing friends and the most extroverted historians. Chloe said it would be going out three times a week, pre-drinks central and no pressure to eat or spend much time together if you wanted to spend some nights elsewhere.

To my surprise I found that I had changed, really changed and I didn't know why. I didn't want to live in that environment anymore, I felt sick of it, I didn't want to be judged on how drunk I got, how outgoing I was, and how many people I slept with. I craved steadiness and close friendship, not extravagance. I turned down Chloe's offer, to her shock, and I could tell we were never going to be close again. Her eyes stung with betrayal and I realised I'd really hurt her these last few weeks. We were no longer best friends. The next day she told the rest of the house she'd found a place for next year and it was just Holly, Anna and I left. Unfortunately, three bedroomed places were even rarer than four and often more expensive. I also wasn't looking forward to living in such a small house with Holly, though Anna assured me she'd forgive me as soon as the stress of finding a place had gone.

A week later Anna invited her Hall CU around to our flat for dinner and I finally met the people she was referring to all the time. Holly seemed a lot happier to be close to me when we were surrounded by strangers. I suddenly became an acceptable lifeline. Fran and Josh were the only people I knew and they seemed completely relaxed in our flat and eager to facilitate easy bonding, though Josh never lost his awkward smile when he spoke to me alone and I realised he was just naturally shy. The bounciest girl I'd ever met with bright pink hair was introduced as Rose. She seemed to have no concept at all of personal space and was always shouting, shrieking, or clapping her hands. She was the sort of girl I would have normally avoided for the plague of social awkwardness and inappropriateness that followed her. However, the new, or perhaps temporary me, who was exploring new ways of thinking, tried very hard not to find her annoying. Very, very, hard. I was amazed at how accepted she was in this group. How people laughed along with her outrageous comments and remarks. It seemed strangely honest somehow.

Then there was the sharp contrast with quiet, Chinese, Mei, who seemed to be closer to Rose than anyone else. I was used to the Asians at Uni keeping to themselves in big huddles, but here, Mei seemed to belong. Her English wasn't even that great, unlike Fran who had been born in England, despite her Malay heritage.

Then there were two jokey boys, Gideon and Joel, who were constantly bouncing off each other, and a more studious looking Chris in grey cardigan and big plastic glasses, the cool nerd look. Something told me he was the new Christian Josh had referred to in the cinema.

After meaningless chatter where I felt I was just trying to keep up with the conversations and include Holly, we sat down for dinner. Anna had cooked roast vegetables with sweet potato and sausages. I'd never had sweet potato before Uni and couldn't get enough of it. It rivalled my last obsession with pesto which was starting to lose its magic. Why hadn't Mum cooked with these things that were so easy and so *good*? I was currently eating a baked sweet potato every single lunch time and still couldn't get enough.

As Anna served up, Rose squealed in delight. "Anna, you are a-maze-ing. Like, I sooo wish I could cook like you."

Anna just laughed at her. "This is easy! Just bung it in the oven for an hour."

Rose sighed theatrically. "Never works like that for me." Mei patted her shoulder sympathetically. She noisily smelt her plate as it was put before her. "Capital, capital!" she announced in a strange accent I couldn't place. Everyone else at the table laughed. Was that an in joke or were they just laughing at her craziness?

Everyone got quieter as we started to eat. I made small-talk to Holly, glad she was starting to soften to me again. Then, as the boys finished their plates first, their gentle but noisy banter grabbed all the attention. I found out Joel was a guitarist in a band and that Gideon was constantly teased for being late to everything. While they were laughing loudly, I leant over to quietly speak with Josh.

"I read your book, and a few others," I said in a low voice. I noticed Anna listening closely, while pretending not to.

"What did you think?" he asked between mouthfuls.

"I don't know," I said truthfully, yet not wanting to offend these nice Christians, and their still crazy-seeming delusions. "I was hoping they would help me understand Christianity, but I still don't understand at all. I was hoping that if God existed he would have made it obvious through those books. I was hoping for one of those lightning bolt moments."

Josh smiled at me and his posture was reassuring. "Those books are only meant to break down barriers which stop people wanting to explore Christianity. They show it's logical and break down misconceptions. The best place to meet Jesus and hear God speak to you is the Bible. The whole book is God revealing Himself to us."

I frowned. "But I don't know a thing about the Bible. I can't understand it when I read it."

"That's all right," came Fran's London accent. I hadn't even noticed her listening. "We can go through it together, or with Anna. It just takes a bit of practice and it doesn't matter if you don't understand everything first time around."

I nodded, cautiously. "Ok."

"We can meet up after Events Week if you want to. You might have some of your questions addressed at the talks next week. Anna and Rose here are sharing their testimonies on Wednesday evening. Then there is a course for those wanting to find out more starting afterwards called 'Christianity Explored'."

Now the whole group's attention was on me and I felt a bit awkward. It was as if they actually thought I would be converted. Their lives were so clearly based on such different things to mine; I would never be like them. They even thought differently. People didn't really change that much when they reached our age.

"So how did you guys all become Christians anyway?" I asked to get the attention off myself. I felt Holly sink lower in the seat next to me as if she thought it would help her escape the conversation. I looked at Josh to start.

"Eh, well, I grew up in a Christian family. My parents took me to church every week and I went to Sunday school. However, it wasn't until I went on a camp when I was about ten, that I realised what it really meant. Until then I thought it was all about rules and how well you remembered Bible stories. And I was all right with that. I knew all the stories in Sunday school that we did again and again and I knew that if I followed the rules, people would think I was a nice person. When I was ten, I realised for the first time it wasn't about rules at all. It wasn't about what I'd done, but about what Jesus had done. I realised it was impossible to follow all the rules, and that was my biggest problem, but Jesus had followed them for me, then taken the punishment I deserved. The punishment for all the times I'd messed up and hurt people. Therefore, I just had to accept what He had done for me. I didn't have to earn forgiveness by 'being good' as I never could. I didn't have to feel lost in guilt every time I did something wrong. This changed my life. I no longer had the aim of wanting everyone to think well of me. I was free from other people's opinions because the only one that really matters is God's, and He sees Jesus' perfect life when He sees me."

I'd never really thought of Christianity like that. Surely it was still all about rules even after Jesus' death? Josh smiled over to Anna to be the next.

She looked at her hands on the table and then smiled nervously at me. "My parents were also Christians but I openly rebelled against their faith. I didn't want to be branded 'weird' by all my friends. My dad is a vicar and so I felt a lot of pressure to be the 'good vicar's daughter' by the town community as if that was my whole identity. So I rebelled against that, I didn't find it fair. Things peaked when I stole my dad's car to drive to a party when I was fourteen and crashed it by accident. Luckily none of us were hurt but my parents' trust was broken which made things worse. I felt like I didn't belong to their family. My older brother got perfect grades at school which made me angrier. Two weeks after I crashed the car I got expelled from school for smoking and drinking instead of being in class. I felt really rubbish, but I was angry at everyone else except myself."

Anna paused to smile at my shocked expression. I couldn't imagine gentle, bouncy Anna doing any of that stuff. It was as if she'd been a completely different person. I realised how little I knew her. All the other people had clearly heard this before and I thought how nice it would be to belong in such a tight-knit group.

Anna continued. "Then a school friend who also had Christian parents asked me to go to this camp with her. I was so bored, I couldn't wait. And there, unbelievably, I met Jesus, through the talks and studying the Bible. He completely changed my life and restored my relationship with my parents, who are the most forgiving people I've ever known, even if we still have our disagreements." She smiled. "Rose, you next."

I was still in a state of shock. How? How had she met Jesus? How had she changed so much?

Rose for once looked serious. "My parents aren't Christians. I was sent to boarding school when I was, like, eleven and hated it. People were very unfriendly and used to leave me out of everything. I wasn't 'cool' enough for anyone to, like, even be associated with me, you know? I asked my parents if I could leave but they said I had to stay and work out how I could fit in, that it would make me strong and independent and all that. They took a massive step back to 'help' me become self-sufficient so I was only seeing them two or three times a year. I felt very lonely. Then I was invited to the school CU. For the first time I found people who not only talked to and included me, but, like, proper loved me and accepted me. I had never met Christians before, so spent a year, like, completely confused by what they believed. However, I really badly wanted to be part of that group so I kept on staying and trying hard to understand. I became a Christian at thirteen and realised my parents were wrong when they believed independence was the way to strength. I realised that I could be weak and utterly depend on Jesus and that gave me everything I needed to face the world. Jesus provided me with the best family I could ever have!" She suddenly grabbed Mei and Joel and squeezed them into her. "Who's next?" she squealed.

I found Rose's story strangely moving. I was so happy these people had accepted her. I felt so guilty for my natural reaction to push her away where she couldn't annoy me. The way I felt like counting the number of 'likes' in every sentence. We could naturally be so mean!

"I'm from China and also went to boarding school," said Mei with a heavy accent. "In my school, you're not allowed to try to convert somebody to Christianity and you can get expelled for owning a Bible. I'd not heard what it was about. I just thought it was part of Western culture. But my roommate had a Bible and when it was night time she'd tell me the stories from it and sometimes read it aloud to me." She paused to make sure she had been understood. Fran gave her a nod and she continued. "At first it was just exciting to do something forbidden, but then I realised Su Ling really believed it and that it was important. I became a Christian and she explained everything she knew to me. Then we'd try to tell other people. It was really nice when I came here and found that people believed exactly the same thing. That God is the same here as He is in China."

Fran mentioned her story was very similar to Josh's and raised an eyebrow at Chris. He shrugged and pushed his glasses further up his nose. "I still haven't really put my thoughts in order but three months ago I was an atheist and now I'm a Christian." He smiled as if he couldn't believe it himself. "When I realised what Jesus had done for me, well you can't ignore that, can you? If somebody's died for you, that requires some sort of response. Now it's suddenly like everything in the world makes more sense. It's like I finally understand, you know?"

Joel put his arm on Chris' shoulder. "Now you're stuck with us for eternity, hey, mate? What on Earth have you let yourself in for?" They joked and jostled for a few seconds. Then Joel turned to me. "I'm not sure when I became a Christian. Happened when I was very young. Had a few rebellious years as a teenager but realised that that stuff only leads to pain and confusion. I realised Jesus' way genuinely is the best way. Been better since. Your turn, Gids."

Gideon shrugged awkwardly. "I believe in God, like my parents, but not really in the same way as these guys. I suppose I'm still just figuring things out. I'm just a bit lazy," he grinned sheepishly. "But I'll make up my mind eventually. I believe Jesus was God, but struggle with most of the rest of the Bible, like Revelation and Old Testament stuff."

"Do you want to share your testimony, Izzy?" asked Fran. She caught me completely off guard. Non-Christians don't have these 'testimony' things, as they called them.

I thought about Sarah and about Mike. "No, thanks. I don't know what I think on anything yet."

For the rest of the evening I quietly studied the Hall CU, trying to put my finger on the root of what was different about them. They introduced me to a game called 'Boggle Head' where you put a pedometer on your head and competed to get the most steps in a minute by just manically nodding your head. It was one of the funniest things I'd even seen and I laughed harder than I had in months. Then we played a game called 'Fish Bowl' which was similar to 'Charades', and my favourite game which was 'Chinese Charades'. It was a mixture of 'Chinese Whispers' and 'Charades' where you pass a scene on to the next person by acting in silence, who then acts it to the next person and so on. The other team get to watch it stray further and further from the truth in hysterics. The last person then had to guess what the original scene was and was always very wrong. Even Holly enjoyed it.

If there was one thing I could admit about Christians, it was that they had fun games.

"Love that surpasses all knowledge."

Chapter Ten

The next day I found all of Anna's Hall CU friends on Facebook and added them. As they accepted my requests, I realised they were all as bonkers as I'd feared. Almost all of them had a profile picture advertising their Events Week and their cover photo was the program of all the lunch time and evening talks. I just couldn't work it out. Didn't they care what other people thought? *All* of their friends saw their Facebook page. How could they be fine with other people rejecting their open invitations? Thinking they were weird? Didn't that shake them to their very core? How could this Events Week mean so much to them? How could they be so desperate for people to come? It was such a different mindset to mine I found it fascinating. I could only have pictures on Facebook of me looking fun and beautiful. How could they not care?

I glanced up at Sarah over the rim of my laptop. "You would have loved it here, Saz," I whispered to her. "You would have loved to be surrounded by these people and organising these events." Silence. I imagined her voice. "I know, I know you want me to go." I smiled. And I had thought Anna's friends were weird and here I was arguing with a photo.

I was really behind with work so for the remainder of the

week I spent almost every minute outside of lectures, netball and flat meals working. The essays weren't the best I'd ever written, but the arguments I was representing just seemed so meaningless and petty next to the ones going around my head. Is there a God? If there is can I know him? Is there such a thing as right and wrong? Why is there suffering? Can your life be based on better things than what people think of you and what you can achieve? There had to be more to your identity than that.

Then Monday came and Events Week was on top of me everywhere I looked or went. Suddenly the streets were filled with people in bright red hoodies and a vaguely Christian caption on the back, like moving adverts. Where had all these Christians sprung from? It was like the launch of a previously underground revolution. On every corner I was handed a flier for the talks happening that day and people shouting '*Free lunch! Free dinner*!' In the ASS library I evaded Christians doing questionnaires to ask people what they believed. In our one lecture of the morning Laura even stood at the front of the year and invited them to the talk that lunch. She shook as she said it, looking so small in her bright red hoodie, but you could tell she meant it.

At the end of the lecture both Laura and Anna were waiting as if in ambush to see if I would go to the lunch time talk. Anna already had one medic friend in tow. I nodded and said I would try to go to them all and I thought Anna would burst from happiness. I almost felt guilty for giving her false hope. I didn't want to give her the false impression that I was actually going to become a Christian and change as completely as she had.

All the talks were packed which I hadn't been expecting. Some of them ran out of seats so the Christians all stood in a red line at the back or left the room to reappear mysteriously at the end. The lunch time talks were in the physics or medics' lecture theatres and big baguettes were handed out on the door. The evening talks were held in the basement of a church in the middle of the University called 'Woodies' or at the Student Union. They involved hot food before the talk and live music at the end played by Christian students. Everything felt surreal, this strange bubble of excitement from people who were so often ignored and were finally being listened to.

I didn't want to admit it to Laura or Anna but I found the talks very confusing at times. There were names from the Bible I knew nothing about and verses that were emphasised and I wasn't always sure why. Some things really struck me, however. These people genuinely believed that the Bible was backed by overwhelming evidence. They didn't believe it could be replaced by science or that they contradicted each other. In fact, most of the Christians seemed to be engineers, medics and other scientists, while the humanities were under represented. They believed we were all going to Hell if we didn't follow Jesus. They believed Christianity wasn't just a religion of tradition but an active relationship with God. They, like C.S. Lewis in 'Surprised by Joy', believed He was the only place you could get true satisfaction in life. And the thing that was repeated again and again was 'grace', which apparently meant you didn't earn going to heaven by being a good person but that it was a free gift. It wasn't about rules. I found this the most confusing bit of all. They could say they were saved before they followed rules, but then they still had to follow rules to be a Christian didn't they?

The last talk surprised me the most. I'd even found myself taking notes. It was all about the historical accuracy of the accounts of Jesus' life that were in the Bible. As a historian I'd finally felt myself on familiar ground and had to agree the speaker made some very good points. From within the texts themselves we had four accounts from either eyewitnesses or, in Luke's case, gathered from eyewitnesses. All had been written in the lifetime of those who would have been able to dispute the stories if they had been untrue, including over five hundred people who had met Jesus after he'd been raised from the dead. The whole way through, the names and addresses and professions of those who the events had occurred to were mentioned, as if the author expected you to go and find them if you doubted his account. Dates and places were given. Random details were sometimes included. I realised that these stories had never intended to be fairy tales, they were written as accounts. At the time these had been written it would have been easy to prove them wrong if they were incorrect.

Then there were the events themselves. Jesus had performed miracles and teachings in front of thousands. The disciples, who had known Jesus better than anyone, went from being terrified at Jesus' death, to being willing to be tortured, imprisoned and horrifically killed for their faith once they had seen Him risen. If they hadn't believed Jesus was God and that He was worth dying for, there was no way they could have endured what they went through. Then there was how fast the message spread after Jesus' death. If it hadn't really occurred, how could you explain the thousands who quickly became Christians across the Middle East and parts of Africa and Europe within the lifetime of the events? Especially all the non-Jews who didn't even have a strong cultural link. Then the fact that even though the letters and accounts that formed the Bible spread to all these different places far away from each other, the literature stayed exactly the same in each one, showing nobody was tampering with it. It hadn't been subject to literary Chinese Whispers or it would have changed differently in each one. It must have been copied and handed down accurately. I found it fascinating.

Then there was a man who had been persecuting the Christians, who was rich, intelligent and on an incredible career path. He suddenly met the resurrected Jesus and then gave up everything he had by becoming a Christian. He'd changed his name to Paul and started to tell people what he had seen and so became an outcast, beaten, tortured, imprisoned, shipwrecked and finally beheaded. Nobody would go through that unless they were absolutely sure. Why hadn't they said stuff like this in religious studies at school? In religious studies all the grand arguments had just been from human reason for the existence of God. Purely using human logic to prove him instead of looking at the evidence God himself had given. Things like Jesus and the Bible. We hadn't done either in school. No wonder the arguments then had always seemed so detached. It was like the conclusion he was a product of the human mind was inescapable as the arguments had been dreamt up from the human mind in the first place.

By the end of the week I was almost as exhausted as Anna and Laura who had both spent time handing out flyers and making sandwiches. They had gotten up early to have breakfast with the CU and pray every morning and stayed late at the evening talks to help clear up. I'd stayed a few times to stack the chairs, feeling sorry for them. Anna had even skipped some of her lectures, which she never normally did. I couldn't believe all these students had given up so much of their time and so much money to get people to these talks.

At every talk we'd been given a flyer for Christianity Explored. It was a course to explore things further in groups. Anna excitedly declared over sixty non-Christians had said they were interested off the back of the week. However, I didn't want to go to a big group where they could set the agenda and there could be peer pressure. I wanted Fran and Anna to teach me. I wanted to be free to ask as many questions as I wanted and to analyse the bits I chose without feeling I was being disruptive.

That Sunday I was drinking tea by myself in our kitchen and thinking about what it must have been like to live in the days of Jesus. Anna entered with Fran as she often did after church. They always walked or got lifts there and back together and discussed deep questions. Fran beamed when she saw me and gave me a hug. Anna put the kettle back on and asked me what I had thought of the talks.

"Interesting," I replied, still just sipping my tea. "I certainly learnt some new things." I knew she wanted to hear more about what I thought about God and whether I was starting to believe, but I didn't think I was starting to and I didn't want to upset her after all the hard work she'd put in.

"Do you have any questions?" pushed Fran.

I nodded, wondering if it would come across as sly. They seemed like they'd been ignoring the Old Testament and I was wondering if they were ashamed by it. "Why were almost all the bits of the Bible talked about and quoted from, from the books about Jesus? And the books written after? Why were none from the Old Testament?"

"Two reasons," said Fran, holding up two fingers as she came to sit opposite me, crossing her dainty legs. Her London accent never seemed to suit the delicate way she moved and dressed. Anna stayed making the tea. "One, from an historical accuracy point of view, it's much easier to prove the historical accuracy of the Gospels than the older books, purely because they were more recent and so we have more copies of the text, more complementary accounts from non-Christians. When we're talking to non-Christians who want to know why they should trust the Bible, it's easiest to start there. Then if they accept what Jesus says, they can see how He took the Old Testament literally and saw it as relevant. He says He is the King who was promised by the Old Testament, He fulfils it, is a continuation of it, so then we can take the Old Testament seriously as well. Izzy, the Bible says the same thing over and over again so is one continuous story. The Old Testament is full of constant predictions of Jesus, which if you see how they are fulfilled first, then helps to validate the texts they're in from hundreds of years before." She lowered a finger. "And secondly. If you're wanting to investigate God, what better place to start than when He was down here on Earth, speaking to us, face to face. It's clearer with Jesus than anywhere else."

I nodded. "That makes sense. But isn't the Old Testament very different from the New? Isn't it all God judging people and genocide and polygamy and things? Doesn't Jesus seem very different from that God by speaking against violence and telling us all to love and accept one another? It doesn't seem at all consistent."

Fran smiled as if reassuring me it was all right to ask my questions. She seemed so confident in her faith, as if she'd thought through all this hundreds of times before. No wonder Anna looked up at her. I hoped I would end up as comfortable in my beliefs at the end of all this, wherever I landed. "God is the same all the way through. He is consistent. The way I find it the easiest to understand is that the patterns throughout the Bible help us understand God's nature. One pattern that repeats itself again and again is how God deals with people. Firstly, He blesses them and tells them the best way they can live. Then they ignore and dishonour God. Sometimes this happens over

142

generations, sometimes only a matter of hours. Then He warns them and gives them a chance to repent, which means to say sorry and correct their behaviour. He is full of mercy. Sometimes He gives them several warnings and several chances. Then those who continue to do terrible things and ignore God, He punishes as He brings about justice."

She paused to remove her cardigan and to check I was following by gauging my expression. I nodded for her to continue. "This is the same pattern in the New Testament. We had previously rejected God. Jesus came with a warning and a chance to repent, but this time with a permanent solution, the crescendo of the whole Bible. This is the last time this pattern needs to repeat. When Jesus took our place by dying for us He dealt with sin once and for all. Those who accept His sacrifice are now represented by Jesus' perfect life, rather than their own sinful one. God sees them as perfect. No more patterns of failure. It works because this arrangement between God and us depends just on God, not on our own actions. We can't mess this one up like we kept on doing in the past. We just have to believe and repent, turning away from the things in our life that aren't consistent with our new, restored relationship as God's adopted children.

"But of course there is the final stage of the final pattern, the stage of judgment on those who haven't listened. We just haven't had it yet. Jesus talked more about Hell than any other person in the Bible. His warning was very real. It's not that the New Testament has moved on from Judgment, in fact it shows how terrible what we have done is. The fact that Jesus had to be tortured, die for us, and be separated from God on that cross, as all God's wrath was poured out on Him, shows what a serious position we are in. That was what we all deserve! Just as the Old Testament gives us many foretastes of God's final judgment and how terrible it will be, it is also a warning for us today. It hammers into our head how serious sin is and what it leads to so we understand more how much we need Jesus. It's all linked. The Old Testament is a foretaste of the New, continuing to today and onto the future."

I shifted uncomfortably as Fran thanked Anna for bringing her tea. "It just sounds horrible to me."

Fran nodded. "I know it can. But just because you don't like something, doesn't make it not true." She paused to study me. "We live in a society where we're constantly told to big ourselves up, see ourselves as special. We're told we can do anything we set our hearts to. That we are each amazing and that we should never doubt ourselves." She paused again. "While it is true we have tremendous worth, far more in fact than society believes, it is also true that we do so many things that are wrong. We're broken on a global scale. And we can't help but be selfish and hurt other people. We constantly compete with those around us to be better than them. Our hearts are so corrupt that it is impossible for anyone to live a perfect life; we even mess up against our own will. We all have so much evil in us. That's not what society tells us, that we are weak and destructive. But it doesn't take much to realise it's true. Just look at the world around us. We've rejected God, who made us for Himself. Then, even though He already owned us, He died to buy us back from the mess we made. Can you imagine how serious it is to throw that sacrifice back in His face? God can't stand evil; He hates what we do to each other. He is being so merciful in keeping this gap between warning and judgment, but at the end of the day, evil must be destroyed."

I felt deeply uncomfortable with this conversation. It still felt very different in tone to a lot of the Christian conversations

I'd had. It felt so dark and terrible. Fran must have read my expression. "Look up Ezekiel 16, if you have a moment, Izzy. It will help you understand how God sees our sin and how serious it is. It's an Old Testament passage for you."

I nodded and put those thoughts to one side to examine later. I tried to return to the reasons I'd started this conversation in the first place. I still felt that the Old Testament was the key to helping me dismiss Christianity. "Fran," I said eventually. "You know you said you'd read the Bible with me. Well can we not do one of those eyewitness accounts of Jesus? Can we do an Old Testament book?"

Fran beamed at me. "Of course. One of the Old Testament books doesn't even mention God's name, yet you can still learn so much about Him when you look. It's called Esther and is quite short. Does that sound acceptable?"

Right, God. I've listened to your Christians, been to your Events Week, and now I'm reading your Bible. If you really exist, I expect you to start speaking to me.

I excused myself and worked all afternoon until evening but Fran's words and confidence wouldn't leave me alone. *Ezekiel*, I was sure that name rang a bell. I was sure I'd seen something about it in Sarah's diary. I changed and got ready for bed, then snuggled under the covers with just my bedside lamp on. I fished the bound case out from under the bed and, pulling the duvet up to my chin, flicked through.

There it was. A double page filled with doodles that were dark and sorrowful rather than her normal colourful flowers and suns and people dancing. Here there were ragged women and crying eyes and smoking cups. That's why I'd noticed it before. There were two different Bible passages written out on either page and spanning both pages at the bottom was a prayer. On the left was Ezekiel 16, exactly the passage Fran had recommended to me. On the other was part of Luke 22. Maybe it was a strange coincidence Ezekiel 16 was here or maybe it was just a really popular Bible passage, I didn't know.

So this was going to help me understand my sin according to Fran. I read Ezekiel 16 quietly out loud to help me concentrate.

"'On the day you were born your cord was not cut, nor were you washed with water to make you clean, nor were you rubbed with salt or wrapped in cloths. No one looked on you with pity or had compassion enough to do any of these things for you. Rather, you were thrown out into the open field, for on the day you were born you were despised.

"'Then I passed by and saw you kicking about in your blood, and as you lay there in your blood I said to you, "Live!" I made you grow like a plant of the field. You grew and developed and entered puberty. Your breasts had formed and your hair had grown, yet you were stark naked.

"'Later I passed by, and when I looked at you and saw that you were old enough for love, I spread the corner of my garment over you and covered your naked body. I gave you my solemn oath and entered into a covenant with you, declares the Sovereign Lord , and you became mine.

"'I bathed you with water and washed the blood from you and put ointments on you. I clothed you with an embroidered dress and put sandals of fine leather on you. I dressed you in fine linen and covered you with costly garments. I adorned you with jewellery: I put bracelets on your arms and a necklace around your neck, and I put a ring on your nose, earrings on your ears and a beautiful crown on your head. So you were adorned with gold and silver; your clothes were of fine linen

and costly fabric and embroidered cloth. Your food was honey, olive oil and the finest flour. You became very beautiful and rose to be a queen. And your fame spread among the nations on account of your beauty, because the splendour I had given you made your beauty perfect, declares the Sovereign Lord.

"'But you trusted in your beauty and used your fame to become a prostitute. You lavished your favours on anyone who passed by and your beauty became his. You took some of your garments to make gaudy high places, where you carried on your prostitution. You went to him, and he possessed your beauty. You also took the fine jewellery I gave you, the jewellery made of my gold and silver, and you made for yourself male idols and engaged in prostitution with them. And you took your embroidered clothes to put on them, and you offered my oil and incense before them. Also the food I provided for you—the flour, olive oil and honey I gave you to eat—you offered as fragrant incense before them. That is what happened, declares the Sovereign Lord.

"'And you took your sons and daughters whom you bore to me and sacrificed them as food to the idols. Was your prostitution not enough? You slaughtered my children and sacrificed them to the idols. In all your detestable practices and your prostitution you did not remember the days of your youth, when you were naked and bare, kicking about in your blood."'

I was frozen in shock; I hadn't been expecting that, not at all. God saw me as His beloved wife who was blatantly cheating on him. I realised my hand was shaking as so many memories that I'd locked up tight came back. The memories of so much pain when it turned out my dad had been sleeping with other women, just as Mum found out she was pregnant again with Jack. It had literally torn our family apart. Mum had been screaming and screaming at Dad and then I hadn't seen her smile for weeks. Granny had had to come over to help look after us. After that I'd never spoken to Dad again. Not after all the pain he had caused. Jack had never met him.

I was crying as all that buried pain erupted out of me. I'd been too young to understand what was going on and process things at the time, but it was so painful to look back on now.

After ten minutes or so I managed to drive myself out of the past and concentrate again on what was before me. I had vowed that no matter whatever happened I would never cheat on anyone, especially in a long term relationship. It was so wrong, so selfish, so hurtful. In my eyes it was one of the worst things you could do. Yet God said that was how He felt about me. That I was meant to be promised to Him yet just took what He gave me and excluded Him, made a mockery of Him, cheated on Him. If God was real and I had hurt Him so badly, how would He ever forgive me? Then another part of me rose up and rebelled against it. Come on, Izzy, you've never been *that* bad. He couldn't really feel like this, could He?

My eyes flicked to the passage that Sarah had linked this one to. Luke 22: 39-44:

'Jesus went out as usual to the Mount of Olives, and his disciples followed him. On reaching the place, he said to them, "Pray that you will not fall into temptation." He withdrew about a stone's throw beyond them, knelt down and prayed, "Father, if you are willing, take this cup from me; yet not my will, but yours be done." An angel from Heaven appeared to him and strengthened him. And being in anguish, he prayed more earnestly, and his sweat was like drops of blood falling to the ground.'

This one I found more confusing. What was Jesus in anguish about? What was the 'cup' being given to Him? I needed some sort of context.

Still feeling very emotionally unstable I went down to Sarah's prayer at the bottom, hoping it would help me piece it all together.

'*Father,*

I am so sorry for the way I've treated our relationship, how I've not always thought it the most precious thing to me. I'm sorry I've so often taken it for granted and so cheapened it. Thank you that you took and accepted me when I had nothing to give back. Thank you for your overwhelming generosity and love. After reading and thinking through Ezekiel 16 I see how I have so often done those things. I see how I have taken the good gifts you lovingly gave me and chosen to worship them instead, my family, my intelligence and success at school, my holidays. Those times I ignored you or acted as if other things were more important when you had given me everything! How can I have been so foolish and unfaithful! I think about how awful I have been then look at what you did to win me back. Jesus died for me in anguish all because I had been unfaithful and ungrateful. You died to take the consequence of my actions so I could come back freely with the evil left behind me. You forgave me utterly and completely just because I asked. Then I look at how scared and anxious you were before you were arrested to be killed, just from contemplating what was going to happen. How you knew exactly what was coming and were so stressed you sweated tears of blood. Yet you still thought I was worth it. Your unfaithful, cheating wife. You still took the punishment on my behalf. Oh, Jesus, thank you. I know I could never repay you and that you don't want me to try. I am so grateful for what you did, the pain it cost you, after how much I'd hurt you! I could just never imagine it! But I will praise you for the rest of my life, and then all eternity for it. I will try to love you as a faithful wife should love her husband. I will try to remember your overwhelming, enduring love surrounds me every day and to stop looking for satisfaction elsewhere.

Thank you.'

I stared at the diary unable to physically swallow. My whole body felt tense. For the first time in my life I think I understood what Jesus had done for me. I understood why the Events Week had been so focused around His life. I flicked back to the sentence scrawled on the inside front cover. Sarah was right. If this was true, Jesus' cross did change everything. Had He really died for me?

"He lifts his voice, the Earth melts."

Chapter Eleven

Holly walked triumphantly into the kitchen where Chloe, Anna and I were cleaning to Disney music. I was attempting to clean the oven but had no idea how to get off such thick grime.

"I've found a house!" she announced. "Somebody in my year had a last minute drop out which almost stopped them signing so I accepted straightaway. We signed this afternoon."

"Oh," said Anna, looking taken aback. "I thought we were going to get one with the three of us."

Holly tossed her hair defensively. "Well you guys didn't seem to be contributing much. I saw a space and didn't want to be the one left with the scraps. I'm sure finding a house that can squeeze you in won't be too hard." She strode from the room, leaving us speechless. Anna paused and then ran after her, concerned.

I felt so guilty. It was my fault her initial, perfect housing plan was messed up, and now she was going to have to live with people she probably barely knew. I scrubbed the oven harder and Chloe paused to lean down over me.

"You, okay, Izzy? Want to tell me what's going on in that head of yours? You used to let me in. You still feeling rubbish about Mike?"

Now she said it, I realised I hadn't thought about Mike in days. I sat back on my knees and sighed, flexing my shoulders. "No, I'm not sure I am anymore. I just needed to step back a bit and see myself. I wanted to see why I was doing and thinking what I was. I realised I was trying too hard to be accepted and fit in."

Chloe lightly rested her hand on my shoulder. "And now? You going to start coming out again? Do you even know who you might live with?"

I shrugged. "I don't know yet. But I'm already starting to feel a bit better about myself, like I can defend the ground I stand on."

Chloe shrugged and started to shake off her cloth in the bin. "I'm glad you're finding yourself. Got to be true to yourself and all that Pixar cheese."

What did that saying even mean? Who was I? And surely what I was was just a product of localised culture telling me which desires to express and which to suppress. I was probably a girl who needed to get drunk and dance provocatively to feel accepted and like I was having fun. I didn't want to be true to myself and all my failings. I wanted to be true to something better, something that meant more. I wanted to be true to something that didn't make right and wrong depend on what mood I was in or what current sympathies my culture had. I wanted to stand on something that couldn't be shaken or removed and feel secure in that. But it had to be true, beyond a doubt. I'd never based my life on anything I'd really thought was true. Maybe that's why I felt so lost in questions that had no answers.

"That house with Anna's friends still got two spaces?" asked Chloe.

I shrugged. "That was two weeks ago. Either they must

have found two other people or they would have lost the house by now. They probably got a house with just them."

Anna came back into the room looking drained. "No, it's still available. It's owned by a couple at my church so it's not through an agency or anything. There are quite a few potential takers for those two spaces so they've been waiting to see who needs it the most."

I stretched my aching back. "If it's meant for Christians, you should join with another of your friends, Anna. I can find somewhere else. You've been very kind waiting for me."

Anna laughed. "Don't be silly, of course you should come with me. Sophie, the historian isn't a Christian either. It's not meant for just Christians! And you'll be able to go to lectures with Sophie and Laura. The other people you've met as well; Fran, Mei and Rose."

I thought about it for a moment and then asked sheepishly, "You guys wouldn't expect me to become a Christian?"

"That's a decision between you and God, though we'd happily answer your questions." Anna grinned. "There seriously wouldn't be any pressure."

"So if I met up with Fran but then decided Christianity wasn't true, people wouldn't feel awkward or let down?"

Anna laughed. "There's no strings attached. You make us sound like a press gang. Just be yourself."

"Well, great! But only if those guys want me." I suddenly felt a huge weight off my shoulders I hadn't even realised was there. I felt accepted again. Then that led to the return of guilt again. I stood on tiptoes to put away the oven cleaner. I was just going to let it soak for a while. Chloe had wandered off, I assumed to the bathroom. She always had had a thing about feeling ridiculously dirty after house cleaning and needing a shower. "Is Holly all right?" I asked quietly.

Anna shook her head. "I'm not completely sure. I've said we'll have to go around each other's houses a lot. She partially felt in the way of us moving into this house I think. The people she's moving in with seem nice from what she said." Anna paused, thinking through what she was going to say next. "Holly has had some bad experiences with Christians in the past, Izzy, so I'm pretty sure she didn't want to end up in that house."

I frowned. "What bad experiences?"

Anna looked uncomfortable. "It's not really for me to say, but seems like there were some Christians, or people claiming to be, back where she grew up that said some rather insensitive things to her and her mum. It's really put Holly off. She really hates me talking about it."

I felt a strange sense of seeing something completely differently than before. I was seeing Sarah and my relationship from the other side. I rested my hand on Anna's shoulder. "Don't worry; she may just need time before she's open to listening. It's what I needed. I had a friend who tried for years and I used to cut her off. Looking back I was quite harsh to her without even realising it."

Anna blushed slightly and smiled. "Thanks, Izzy. I'll text the girls about the house."

*

Fran offered to treat me in Boston Tea Party for our first instalment of Esther and I came straight from studying in the ASS library. I was feeling thoroughly down after reading about the Great Depression in America and how meaningless and cheap so many lives became as a result. It was nice to be walking in the spring sunshine and seeing the daffodils pushing out of the flower beds around the roads, filling the grey streets with colour. Even the people were becoming more colourful as skirts and light jumpers started to brave the slight chill.

Fran was waiting outside, texting, and together we ordered and found a seat. I realised I was feeling nervous, both because we were studying something I knew nothing about, and also because I was going to live with Fran next year and I wanted an easy relationship with her. Like most Asians she was slim and graceful and sat straight backed, perched on the edge of the seat. She wore her shiny hair loose and no make-up. She still seemed so certain of herself and confident in this setting. How many people had she taught before me? Where had she learned it all? She smiled at me as we settled down and took out two Bibles; one was brand new with a floral design, the other plain leather and battered. She pushed the new Bible towards me.

"That's for you, from Anna and me. You're going to need it to look into this stuff properly."

I felt myself blush. It felt awkward accepting their gift when they were giving it to me with the aim that I became a Christian. What if I didn't?

"Come on, Izzy, it's not going to bite, it's a present," she said in her matter-of-fact way. "Now, I've put the bookmark in Esther for you as it's a hard book to find."

I opened the book, smelling the fresh scent of paper. Each page was crisp and undamaged unlike Fran's Bible and Sarah's Bible. I opened at Esther and looked up at Fran expectantly; I didn't feel like I'd understand a thing on my own.

"We're going from the beginning to verse twelve. Take your time if you want to reread anything in your head. Stop me if I'm going too fast." She waited for my head nod.

"'This is what happened during the time of Xerxes, the

Xerxes who ruled over 127 provinces stretching from India to Cush: At that time King Xerxes reigned from his royal throne in the citadel of Susa, and in the third year of his reign he gave a banquet for all his nobles and officials. The military leaders of Persia and Media, the princes, and the nobles of the provinces were present.

'"For a full 180 days he displayed the vast wealth of his kingdom and the splendour and glory of his majesty. When these days were over, the king gave a banquet, lasting seven days, in the enclosed garden of the king's palace, for all the people from the least to the greatest who were in the citadel of Susa. The garden had hangings of white and blue linen, fastened with cords of white linen and purple material to silver rings on marble pillars. There were couches of gold and silver on a mosaic pavement of porphyry, marble, mother-of-pearl and other costly stones. Wine was served in goblets of gold, each one different from the other, and the royal wine was abundant, in keeping with the king's liberality. By the king's command each guest was allowed to drink with no restrictions, for the king instructed all the wine stewards to serve each man what he wished.

'"Queen Vashti also gave a banquet for the women in the royal palace of King Xerxes.

'"On the seventh day, when King Xerxes was in high spirits from wine, he commanded the seven eunuchs who served him— Mehuman, Biztha, Harbona, Bigtha, Abagtha, Zethar and Karkas— to bring before him Queen Vashti, wearing her royal crown, in order to display her beauty to the people and nobles, for she was lovely to look at. But when the attendants delivered the king's command, Queen Vashti refused to come. Then the king became furious and burned with anger.'"

Fran paused and smiled quietly at me. I reread the passage again to myself, sieving it through my brain, trying to picture the events, and then met Fran's eyes.

She rested her chin in her hand. "What are your initial thoughts, Izzy?"

I chewed my lip. "Well, it gives a time and a date, like the writer is trying to show this really happened. He gives us information about which king he's talking about so there may have been others of his name. So it's a proper point in history."

Fran nodded. "Go on."

"Well, it's about a rich king who wants to show off his vast wealth by throwing a very big party. He shows off, then there's a feast where everyone gets drunk. It sounds very grand and beautiful. Completely extravagant. Then he wants to show off his wife just because she's beautiful. I assume she realises this so says no. Good for her."

Fran nodded in encouragement. "What do you think about this king?"

I frowned. "I don't like him." Fran smiled and motioned for me to continue. "Well he clearly is obsessed with himself, and money and appearance and good looking women. He just wants people to see him as fun and wealthy by giving them all this free food and wine."

Fran smiled. "Remind you of another culture?"

I paused. "Yes, I suppose it's a lot like ours. Everyone here is obsessed with making themselves more important, making money, and outward beauty. Lots of people show those things off." I paused, thinking over the questions I'd been mulling over for so many months now, wondering if Fran would understand them. "It's something I've been struggling with," I started. "Everyone knows the saying, 'Money can't buy happiness', yet people believe it does all the same. You hear about the rich and famous committing suicide because they feel unsatisfied. If people believe money is not the root of happiness, why is everyone obsessed with making it? Then often people say that money isn't the key to fulfilment, but relationships and families are, like all those cheesy children's Christmas films where the moral is to spend more time with your kids. Or all those romances where you find your 'one true love' and are happy forever after. Yet, at the same time, culture also says it's all right not to commit to other people or have set rules to your relationship as if it doesn't believe they can last. Some say happiness is in independence, even when in relationships, so nobody can be your boss. Nobody but me seems to worry about how much all these ideologies clash even when we're told them again and again every day and everyone just nods along."

Fran nodded. "There is a lot of confusion in our culture, isn't there, Izzy, especially at Uni where everyone's trying to work things out for themselves? I mean, this passage alone can bring two reactions originating from our cultural upbringing, can't it? Our gut reaction, as you said, is 'he's not nice'. Our culture has given us a negative gut reaction against people who flash their wealth and drink to excess and flaunt their partner. Yet on a day to day basis those people are exactly who we celebrate and put on a pedestal. They're the popular people at University. The ones we see as 'living life to the full', they're the celebrities we pay huge amounts of money to and so many people want to be like. We know they've got it wrong, for some reason we disagree with their life, yet we all want to be like them. Our culture simultaneously promotes and denounces them."

I nodded and then looked up sheepishly. "Sorry, I didn't mean to derail our conversation into the philosophy of our culture."

Fran laughed. "Not at all, Izzy. These are exactly the questions the Bible encourages us to ask."

"And you would say that God gives you ultimate satisfaction?" I asked, trying to see things from her point of view. It was easy to poke holes in a system and much harder to find the solutions, as one of my lecturers was always saying.

"That's what Jesus claimed to an outcast woman who'd been married many times and was still searching for fulfilment. He likens himself to 'living water' and offers it to her when all of society has rejected her. If we 'drink' from Him we will never be 'thirsty' again. We will be satisfied. That's what He was saying to her. From a personal point of view though, I'm often not very good at letting Him satisfy me instead of still looking for fulfilment in other areas. I have access to living water but still often drink dirty, finite water anyway. Then I'm always shocked when they let me down." She grinned. "Peter, my boyfriend, is my current temptation for satisfaction. I know God loves me perfectly and never lets me down, but I still want to completely rely on Peter's imperfect love. I put an impossible burden and strain on him. I have to remind myself, that's not fair, Peter isn't God and God fulfils that need so that Peter doesn't have to. When we both rely on God for perfection and not the other, it makes our relationship easier and forgiveness quicker. I shouldn't need Peter to satisfy my deepest needs."

"So do you really, completely, feel one hundred percent satisfied in Jesus?" I tested, leaning forward.

Fran paused and sipped her coffee. "When I'm not trying to put other things in God's place in any particular area, yes I do. Though I have to say I struggle not to do that." She reached a hand out to me. "Though, Izzy, I know it's uncomfortable but I want to stress something. People sometimes purely promote

Christianity as the only way to true satisfaction in this life, but that's not why you need it most. Happiness or satisfaction in this life, even when it's tough, is a bonus. It's something that can help us through tremendous suffering and shows how loving God is, how wonderful our relationship is, the fact He delights in our enjoyment and satisfaction of Him. But the most urgent problem is that if you're rejecting Jesus' sacrifice, there's nothing standing in your defence when you have to face the price for all the wrong you've done in your life."

I nodded. "I read Ezekiel 16, and then about what Jesus did to win me back. I think I can understand more now why it looks so bad to God when we don't follow Him."

Fran leaned across and said slowly, "Izzy, if I may ask, what do you think is stopping you from following Jesus?"

I frowned. I'd never thought of it that way around before. Did I think Jesus was worth following? Yes, especially if He had really died for me in such a horrible way. And everything He did was so good and wise and generous. Did I think following Him would mean giving up too much? Not really. Not anymore when everything had started to feel so hollow and hypocritical and if you really could be satisfied in God alone. I suppose the question was, 'Was it true?' I needed to know beyond a doubt.

"I think I still need God to show me that He's true," I ventured.

"He's done that with Jesus coming in touchable flesh and blood. He's done that in the Bible making more sense of humanity and our world than anything else. He's shown it with prophecies coming true and a book across thousands of years revealing one story about one God," said Fran gently.

I shrugged. "I barely know the Bible. I suppose I feel like if I start to believe it now, I might be caught out by it later when something doesn't add up. I just don't feel like I understand Christianity."

Fran smiled. "You understand our sin. You understand what Jesus did for you, giving forgiveness to you as a free gift so that we can't take any credit. You understand He talks to us through the Bible. You understand that if we follow Him we have eternal life. Izzy; that is enough."

I shuffled back in my seat, not wanting to feel pressured into anything and feeling like she was going too far. "I need to think about it. I need to make this decision properly. Besides, we barely did any of Esther."

Fran smiled. "So we haven't. Next week then?"

I nodded.

Amazing Grace

Chapter Twelve

God wouldn't get out of my head. I was on a dizzying, sickening knife edge of seeing the world in two completely different ways and whichever way I fell would completely determine my future. It was as if nothing in the entire world was certain anymore. I was walking on jelly and sometimes I was feeling like I was drowning as everyone else seemed to balance on it effortlessly above me. I was realising I couldn't be neutral with Jesus. I was either with Him or I had rejected Him. He had really lived. He had claimed to be God. He had claimed to die for us. Was He making it up? Was it true?

I couldn't concentrate in lectures anymore. When writing essays, I would find myself paused mid-sentence, my brain long since strayed elsewhere. I found it hard to talk normally to people. I didn't want to be swayed by people's thoughts. Jesus are you true? Can you actually hear me? Was Sarah right all along? I needed to make a decision. I needed the release of this pressure. I needed Him to give me some sort of sign!

I was walking back into the ASS library to attempt work on my essay, when I noticed Josh in front. He smiled in greeting and opened the library door for me. I thanked him in return.

"You studying here?" I asked. It felt strangely good to see him.

He nodded. "I find the flat too noisy and I've got some big exams coming up."

"Mind if I study with you? I could do with some company." Hopefully having somebody working hard next to me would help me concentrate again.

He smiled and indicated a desk. I dumped my bag and started to unpack the quotes and references for my essay all printed on paper which had long since become screwed up. "What do you study again?" I asked. I wasn't sure I'd ever known.

"Neuroscience," said Josh getting out his laptop. He laughed quietly at my confused expression.

"Is that, like, brain surgery?" I asked.

"No, doctors do that. It's more studying how the brain works. How we form thoughts and memories and emotions."

"Oh." It sounded too far from my areas of expertise to ask anything else. But then I thought about it properly. "Isn't that a hard thing to study as a Christian?"

He frowned. "Not at all. It just makes me amazed at how incredible God is every day." He raised an eyebrow. "Isn't history hard to study as an atheist?"

I smiled. "Agnostic now." I was starting to get used to this reversal of questions by Christians challenging my own beliefs. I was starting to enjoy them. "Why?"

Josh shrugged. "Well all that suffering that would be meaningless and purposeless. The hopelessness of humans doing tremendous evil again and again. Also, if you think about it, we think actions are right or wrong regardless of our culture. For example murder is wrong whether it was committed by us, or committed by a tribal man. So what is the independent source we can calibrate our scale from? We need something outside of cultures, which so often differ from each other and can get it so wrong. Without God as our objective source, 'morality' becomes nothing but a biological adaptation to aid our species' survival. It is utterly culturally dependent and so has no real meaning. There can't really be 'evil'."

I twiddled my thumbs as I tried to stick to my own thoughts rather than get caught in a mostly intellectual argument. "Well it's not very comfortable to think that there's a God who could change all that suffering but who chooses not to," I argued back.

Josh nodded and gave a little smile as he typed in his password and loaded his essay. "The Bible says God is doing things about it. Jesus' sacrifice on the cross gives people a way to find forgiveness and the Holy Spirit gradually helps them rid themselves of the evil in their hearts. Then, when He's patiently waited for long enough for people to have that choice to respond, He'll remake the world pure and perfect with no suffering. Doesn't suffering and death feel wrong to you, Izzy? Doesn't it feel like it shouldn't be there? Doesn't injustice make you angry? How can you explain that? Well that's because suffering shouldn't be there. It's not natural. It's not how creation was made."

I thought about Sarah. Death had been so wrong. It had felt that it should have never happened. But wasn't that just wishful thinking?

Josh must have read my expression unusually well because he backed off immediately. "Sorry, Izzy, I didn't mean to upset you. I'm sorry, that was thoughtless for me to push when I don't know you well."

I waved my hand. "No, that's all right. I... I had a friend who died at school. I miss her, that's all."

164

Josh looked so genuinely concerned I felt like I was going to cry over Sarah all over again, so I tried to smile instead. "Really, it's fine. She was a Christian, so, according to you, she's happy and all that."

Josh stood. "Let me buy you a coffee to make up for it? I usually have one while I work in here."

I nodded and he walked off. Christian boys did seem so different. They seemed more respectful and maybe slightly more cautious, standoffish with girls. I wondered why. Maybe because they would only sleep with one woman, and she had to be a Christian, that meant we became people without the potential for sex. I was his friend, not a potential girlfriend. Though I wondered if Josh was quietly scared of me. How he didn't look me in the eyes for too long and didn't let his body come too close. Maybe he just didn't want to give the wrong message and was nervous because of all these deep conversations.

Josh came back with the coffees and I smiled in thanks, music already playing in my ears. We studied in silence for a few hours and I worked better than I had in weeks. Josh was also writing an essay and every time I got distracted I only had to glance at how much more he'd written than me to be determined to keep up.

When it got to 5:30pm Josh stood up and started to pack. I pulled my ear phones out and asked if he was going back to Durdham. When he nodded I started to pack too so I could walk back with him.

"How are you finding Esther, with Fran?" he asked as he slung his rucksack over one shoulder.

"I like it," I said. "We've had three sessions now. I like how God isn't mentioned and how there's no miracles or anything. Means I can just read it without being sceptical all the time about what actually happened. However, when you look you can see that it's implied that God is working behind the scenes. I find that easier to relate to my life since most of the time it hardly feels like God is right in front of me, like all the bits with Jesus, and I've not seen any miracles or anything." I nodded in confidence. "It's good. Esther's really brave."

We walked out of the door and the icy wind gave us both a shock. Either side of the road in the flower beds, daffodils were braving the weather and forcing themselves up. At their feet, crocuses were more sheltered bursts of colour. The pavements were crowed with huge numbers of students leaving their final lectures, mostly wearing dull browns, greens and navies against the last of winter as it got cold again.

"Izzy," Josh started. "Would you be interested in coming to church?"

I shrugged. Seemed a logical step for the next stage of my journey of exploring Christianity. "They won't mind that I'm not a Christian?"

Josh smiled, which for some reason, made me smile too. "They would love to have you, Izzy. Quite a few non-Christians go."

"Okay. Do you go to the same one as Fran and Anna?" They always came back together at Sunday lunch time.

Josh shook his head. "No, I go to a different one with Rose, Mei and Joel. But they're both good churches and will both welcome you. Go where you're most comfortable."

I nodded. "All right then. I'll see you on Sunday."

*

On Sunday morning I found myself really worried about what I should wear. What length skirt was too short? Could I show my shoulders? How smart should I be? I didn't want to offend anyone but the only time I'd been to church before had been Sarah's funeral and Mum had bought me a smart black dress for it since I'd been a zombie. After I'd changed outfits four times I knocked on Anna's door, made her promise not to laugh at me and then showed her what I was considering. She laughed and said they were all fine and that I could go as casual as I wanted. Then I quickly did my make-up in a subtle look. I was going with a boy after all.

However, the knock on our flat door was from Fran and not Josh. She leant into my room. "Good morning, Izzy. Josh said you were interested in coming to church today and thought it might be better if you came with us instead."

I frowned as I grabbed my handbag. "Why? He said both churches were fine."

Fran shrugged, obviously trying to not make a big deal about it. "He just thought it would be more appropriate."

"Appropriate?" I was really confused. Why was it so hard to read the logic of Christians sometimes?

"Well, you know us two better than Josh and Joel. He thought you'd be more comfortable with girls. He wanted you to feel comfortable."

I shrugged. I would have felt just as comfortable with Josh. To my surprise part of me was a bit disappointed I wasn't going with him. Then again, I was going to be living with these girls next year so it probably was better if I invested in my relationship with them. That was most likely what Josh had been thinking.

It was a forty-five minute walk to church. Anna said they often got a lift from one of the families but hadn't felt they needed one since it was so sunny. For once I didn't feel the need to dominate the conversation with deep questions or

167

comments. That had been so much of my relationship with the both of them. For once it was just good to chat about silly things and to laugh and joke. I found it so refreshing that they never laughed at another's expense or talked behind their backs. Even the lack of swearing and crude joking was strangely nice. I felt out of place yet included all at once.

I found church a very strange experience. I'd never seen so many different ages all together and interacting with each other. There were students I vaguely recognised holding babies or with toddlers on their shoulders. Men and women were intermingled unlike the dinner parties my mum had had. There was a lot of hugging and laughing and a few serious conversations with respectful spaces around them to mark them out. Children ran around shouting. If I hadn't been with Fran and Anna, I would have felt utterly intimidated. I had no idea what the unspoken rules of this place were.

After a welcome from a man wearing a semi casual shirt, we stood up for a few songs I awkwardly just read the words to, while everyone else belted them out, and it acutely reminded me of Sarah's funeral. I was suddenly feeling very emotional and wondered if coming here had been a mistake. Almost unintentionally I reached out for Anna's hand, like I had Sarah's when I felt uncomfortable, and she took it and gave it a squeeze.

Then came the sermon. It was on one of the stories about Jesus, about how a rich man had thought he could be good enough to get into Heaven, but Jesus had said it was impossible for any man, even a rich man (whom the culture saw as blessed by God). It was only possible with God. It was a sad story because the man hadn't been willing to give up his money since he valued it more than God and therefore didn't follow Jesus. The pastor proceeded to explain how we often try to earn the right to go to Heaven instead of accepting it as a free gift due to our pride. For once I felt like I understood what he was saying. Fran had talked about grace before. The gift to go to Heaven was free. Changing your life to please God afterwards was a response in thanks for the enormity of what He had done. It showed you understood God was both king of the world and yourself. It didn't earn salvation.

As everyone around me was praying I tried to think about things logically. If Jesus was offering me a 'get out of jail free' card for nothing because He loved me, I would be mad not to take it. I would be mad to turn down a perfect relationship that was meant to be completely satisfying. Mad to take Hell over Heaven. Mad to value money or sex or career over Jesus. That rich man had been mad to choose Earthly greatness and money over an eternity in Heaven. Had I really been missing such a big choice all my life?

Everyone suddenly stood up and I realised that the prayers had finished and we were singing again. It was 'Amazing Grace'. Finally, a song I knew.

'*I once was lost, but now am found. Was blind but now I see.*'

I'd been feeling so lost and blind. Everyone around me had started to seem lost and blind as well with their wildly different opinions and lifestyles. But never Sarah or Anna or Fran or Josh. I wanted to be able to see. I wanted to be found. I realised I wanted Jesus to be true. I just needed to understand everything. See how everything fitted together. I needed to understand what I needed to do to become a Christian. I needed to check nothing was flawed. I needed to check I understood exactly what Jesus had done on the cross. Then maybe I could accept it as true.

After church, a family invited us to lunch. I didn't know

them at all and expected it to be awkward but actually it was just wonderful to have a proper Sunday roast in an actual home. It felt weird to be reminded that this was what normal life was rather than Halls. We played a card game that involved shouting out the names of objects and the adults were beaten by the eight and nine year old children every time. It was hilarious, especially as the adults tried harder and harder. The father then gave us a lift back to Durdham, while regaling silly stories of his own Uni days.

Anna and I spent the rest of the evening making sausage rolls for the flat and then watching a film with Holly and Chloe. They were both groggy from working all afternoon and happily munched their way through our sausage rolls rather than make any dinner.

The next morning, I decided it would be pointless to go to lectures since my brain was in a whirl. I needed to understand more of the Bible and what it meant to be a Christian. I needed to *know* if it all held together. I kept on feeling like there would be some massive hole just around the corner of where I was.

I went onto the church website and downloaded four sermons from the same guy who'd been speaking. I listened to them while cleaning my bedroom and the bathroom. The rest of the flat was basically deserted. Holly and Anna had almost a full timetable of lectures, Chloe had constant projects that required teamwork in the library and who knew where Mike had started spending all his time. He still wasn't talking to me.

The sermons strangely resonated with me. They were more relevant to day to day life than I'd expected and I found myself thinking after each one how I would be able to change my life to think or act a certain way. They also made sense. They pointed things out about human nature that I'd never noticed before. They explained how the Bible explored our tendencies

170

in thoughts and actions. They described why the Bible gave us the rules and boundaries for our own good. A fish is truly free within the boundaries of the river, where it was safe and healthy, rather than trying to push itself on land. In the same way humans were most free when they stuck within certain moral and practical boundaries. Going beyond those boundaries was just damaging, not true freedom. It actually limited our potential and happiness.

I decided I would start to try to pray. I closed the curtains since it felt more appropriate that way and sat down on my bed.

"God, if you're real and you really love me that much despite knowing what a horrid person I am and have died for me, please show yourself."

I waited in silence for an hour but nothing happened. Disappointed, I opened my curtains and decided I should probably get back to my essay. I was falling so far behind. I probably still didn't understand Christianity enough. I needed to know more.

*

Over the next week I went to the library every day to see if Josh was there since I'd been so effective working with him. However, I only bumped into him once and he seemed to be rushing off somewhere. Part of me wondered if he was avoiding me, but that was stupid since I'd barely bumped into him before.

I tried to catch up with my work and got into the practice of listening to just one sermon a day to limit my time of being distracted by Christianity, but I told Anna I would come to church with her again next week. Chloe seemed curious that I was seriously investigating Christianity and said I had her respect for being so thorough with different world views. She didn't want to discuss it though; she just wanted some help curling the back of her hair.

On Saturday, Anna invited me to a Hall CU meal at Fran and Josh's flat. I happily accepted, grateful to be included and enjoyed the break from work and the silliness of the games. However, it was sad that Josh hadn't been able to come. I wanted to talk about church with him again and try to see how his was different to Fran's. Peter, Fran's boyfriend, was there though. To my surprise they sat at different ends of the table and talked to those around them, even though I noticed sneaked smiles and glances towards each other. Their relationship seemed outwards facing rather than the usual, private affair, and it made me want to study it more closely. Was it easy not sleeping together? How far did they go? Didn't the sexual frustration make them want to rush into marriage?

When dinner was finished and we'd helped with the washing up, I asked Anna where Josh was as we walked back through the corridors to our flat.

"He goes home every other weekend," said Anna. "He has a little sister called Grace. She's his phone background photo. Isn't that cute? She has Down's syndrome. So Josh goes home alternating weekends with his brother to help his parents have some time off and catch up with household stuff. Josh is a bit besotted with her."

I nodded. That was really sweet of him. "What's his brother do?"

Anna paused in front of our door and searched her bag for her keys. "Not sure. Something to do with computers in Exeter or something like that. He's called Joseph. We used to tease Josh that his parents had a massive lack of imagination for choosing such similar names."

I chuckled. The flat corridor was dark and quiet when we entered, a sharp contrast to the bubbly, bright dinner party. I grabbed Anna's hand as she walked away to her room.

"Anna," I started, unsure as to what exactly I was trying to say. "Thank you... for including me and sticking by me. I know I've not given much in return, but I'm really grateful. And for the house. There must have been many other people you would have rather lived with than me. Both you and Fran have given up a lot of time for my questions."

Anna gave my arm a squeeze. "You're more than welcome, Izzy, and I'm definitely looking forward to living with you next year."

*

That Sunday I went to church with Fran and Anna again. Some of the students and people from the week before recognised me and came to talk to me. Laura was there as well this week and seemed so excited to see me at church. She hurriedly introduced me to friend after friend. I realised this was her in her natural environment. Church meant so much to them all.

Monday and Tuesday passed as normal. There was a tension and stress in lectures now as so many students and lecturers started to focus on end of year exams. The essay mark schemes were becoming more and more unforgiving. The stress and tension made me want to spend more time with the Durdham CU who very rarely seemed to discuss exams except in prayer requests. The topic was just getting dull, and I found that I wasn't able to muster the nerves or the feeling that these exams really mattered when there seemed to be bigger questions in the world.

Wednesday I quitted netball. I'd decided that the bitchy attitude and constant comparison of the players was an unhealthy atmosphere to be in, and I no longer wanted to go clubbing with them. I didn't want people to be judging me on my figure or love life anymore. After I sent an email to the team captain, I felt good and spun on my office chair, thinking. Then I decided to Facebook stalk Josh. I wanted to understand him better as the most mysterious member, in my mind anyway, of the CU.

His profile picture showed him playing the guitar in a church band. I hadn't known he played the guitar. It suited him even though he was only half visible behind a singer. He barely had any personal information on there. I found a picture of his brother and him at a wedding, with scarily similar faces but Joseph had much darker hair. Then there was a picture of him cuddling a young girl with almond eyes, I assumed was Grace. He looked so happy in that one. Then hundreds of him in the background at CU events and weekends, or dinners or church with loads of people I didn't know. He seemed so kind and humble. So different from the confidence, witty humour and cool, easy way of Mike. I wondered how much of that was to do with being a Christian.

I decided to go to Fran and Josh's flat again to try Josh's church to see how and why they were different. It was confusing why the Hall CU didn't all share lifts and just go to the same church. It wasn't like they seemed to disagree on many things when they were together. But what did I understand?

I left the flat and walked to the neighbouring block, knocking on their ground floor door. A random flatmate I didn't know let me in and pointed to Fran's, then Josh's door. He mumbled that Fran was out. I smiled as Josh opened his door, hearing the voices.

"Hi, Josh," I started. "Would you mind if we chatted about church again?"

Josh didn't leave his doorway but leant across it, keeping me out. He gave a small smile but underneath he was serious and more awkward than ever. He even shuffled his feet.

He took a deep breath. "Izzy, don't take this the wrong way but, would you mind talking to Fran and Anna about it? I'm sure they would love to."

I folded my arms and raised an eyebrow. This was *definitely* avoiding me.

"Izzy..." he sighed and rubbed his forehead, "I don't... I just don't want us getting closer to have any impact on whether you accept or reject Christianity. I don't want you to be swayed by things other than God and the Bible. I don't want to complicate things."

It took a moment for what he was saying to sink in. I couldn't help but feel a sting of rejection. "But it won't. I'm fine just being friends."

He smiled and raised an arm to comfort me but dropped it when he caught himself. "I'm sorry, Izzy. I just think that maybe it would be more appropriate if you had the deeper conversations with the girls; then nothing gets complicated. Do you see where I'm coming from?"

I paused in the shock of the moment and then I nodded, sulkily. If he didn't want to talk to me, fine! It wasn't like I'd been falling in love with him or anything. I'd just enjoyed talking to him and felt relaxed around him. Now it would just be awkward. "If that's what you think is best," I grumbled. "I would have been fine just talking to you."

I turned to go, annoyed. Josh sighed unhappily and I wondered if I'd somehow hurt him too. That hadn't been my intention. "That may have been the case," he said so quietly I wasn't sure he'd decided whether I should hear or not. "But I'm not sure *I* would have been fine and not been tempted to get closer to you." My eyes snapped back and met his very briefly. "I find you very beautiful, Izzy. I'm sorry but I don't want to be an influence on you."

I nodded, unable to speak as he shut his door. I hurried out of the flat in a daze, reeling with both rejection and affirmation. Great! Now I had another thing to mull over in my head. That had meant Josh fancied me, right? I mentally shook myself. One thing at a time, Izzy. Jesus first, boys second!

"While we were sinners."

Chapter Thirteen

Suddenly it was time to go home for Easter. I was amazed at how quickly the term had gone, yet at the same time, how much I'd changed. At Christmas I'd been falling in love with Mike, now I had barely spoken to him in months. I'd been getting drunk at least twice a week, now I barely even got tipsy. I'd used to measure the curve of my stomach every morning after being in the bathroom and get up half an hour earlier so I could get my hair or make-up just right. Now I often just wore mascara with a bit of concealer. I'd barely noticed myself change, I just... had. I wanted different things now. The world seemed different.

Mum didn't seem to notice much of the difference, but then she didn't see me in many different contexts. For the first time in my life I felt far away from her. She didn't seem to notice the things I couldn't put into words for her. But I realised that was unfair to her. How could she know things I hadn't shown her?

Then again she had changed too in ways I felt left out of. She'd started dating a man called Darren. It was very early stages so she hadn't thought to let me know while I'd been away. Apparently he was an electrician and a good cook. Mum showed me his Facebook photos and asked my opinion. I felt like it would be too self-righteous to say I couldn't tell anything important from his looks alone, despite what I was thinking, so just settled with 'he looks nice.'

After a few days I got a Facebook message from my old school friends, Jen, Claire, Tania, Sue and Beth organising a meet up once we were all back. It felt like a strange lurch back to my old life. Jen's house. Friday. Everyone was to bring one item of alcohol and one snack. I felt both uneasy yet excited to see them all again. I was only beginning to realise how much I'd missed them.

I felt the old routine come back to me easily. The dress that looked inviting yet not too slutty. Perfectly curled hair. Killer heels and bright nails. I even went through the effort of individual fake eyelashes. It could be so much fun dressing up, even if there wasn't much reason to. All I needed was Sarah lying on the bed behind me, visible in the mirror, complimenting yet teasing me at the same time and making ridiculously innocent comments.

Mum drove me to Jen's house with the understanding I could get a taxi home. Technically it was walkable but I wasn't walking twenty minutes in a mini dress while the weather was still cold and didn't want the hassle of carrying extra shoes. Anyway the wind would mess up my hair.

I kissed Mum on the cheek before leaving the car and gave a nonspecific promise of not getting back too late. Mum had invited Darren around for tea tomorrow evening so didn't want me too hung over. I'd explained that I hadn't got that drunk in ages and she just raised her eyebrows in a disbelieving manner. Her reaction had made me sigh and stroppily act just like the teenager I was trying so hard to show her I was not. Why did I only have immature reactions and act moodily when I was at home? Mum was the person I most wanted to prove I was an adult to.

I knocked on Jen's door but they didn't hear through the music so I carefully navigated a flower bed in my heels so I could knock on the window.

Tania opened the door. It felt strange seeing her in the same place, same context as always, even though it had been half a year. She was even more overweight than before. She'd squished herself into a curvaceous corset which left her breasts bulging out to such an extent I was embarrassed and I was a girl! I had to keep glancing down to check the nipple hadn't popped up.

She grinned and gave me a massive hug and I tried not to be awkward about squeezing her. There were no boys here after all, even if I did squeeze her out of her clothes. It would just be a laugh.

A scream from behind announced Jen. She shouted something unintelligible and then almost pushed Tania out of the way to barrel me into a hug.

"Izzy!" she gasped. "You have no idea how bored I've been the last two weeks waiting for all you guys to come home." She wrapped an arm around my shoulder to lead me into the sitting room. "It's so good to see you."

Sue gave me a smile and a wave from the sofa, her skin a ridiculous shade of orange, but her hair and make-up, beautiful. Claire and Beth sat on cushions on the floor next to a bowl of crisps, looking far more normal. Quiet, kind, overly sensitive, but nosey Beth and then Claire who had forever seemed in the background of the group. For once I felt more in common with them than the others.

I sat down and helped myself to a few crisps. "How's University?" I asked Beth. "You were so worried about going."

179

Beth smiled. "I got into Nottingham after all. I had to phone them after results came through and I missed my biology grade. They let me in anyway. I love it there. Met some really nice people."

I beamed. "That's brilliant. All your photos on Facebook are of you looking happy."

Beth nodded. "And how about you?" she asked back.

"Who's this, 'Mike'?" added Claire. "There have been some interesting photos of the two of you."

I looked down, feeling uncomfortable. I didn't know how to explain everything to them. "We're not together any more. He kissed another girl."

Beth put her arm around me looking so sad I thought she might cry herself. "I'm so sorry, Izzy. Sounds like he was an idiot."

Claire nodded in agreement. "It's…"

"Smile!" came Jen's voice, quickly followed by the flash of a camera. She looked at the viewing screen. "Don't you lovely ladies look B.E.A.Utiful?" She flopped down beside me. "But I couldn't help but overhear that you were gossiping without me." She put her hand on top of mine and put her sincere, serious face on. "Izzy. Tell me *everything*."

I shrugged. "I was going out with a guy called Mike for three months and then I ended it after he kissed a girl. I'm over him now."

"That's a shame," said Jen. "Since he looked *gorgeous* on Facebook. Bet he was good in bed?"

"Jen!" I exclaimed. The mood suddenly got uncomfortable. This was the bit where I was meant to say it had been amazing or hint that I was better than him and shame him to get my own back. The bit where I was meant to make everyone insanely jealous of my fabulous private life that couldn't be proven or disproven. I didn't want to play that game anymore. I shrugged.

Jen slapped me playfully. "You're no fun at gossip. We had a scandalous event in our Halls." She raised her voice so that Tania and Sue would listen in too. "It was a secret one. Those up for anything came into this big room and mingled for a bit with music. Then suddenly the lights went off and the rules were *anything went*, if you get my meaning. It was pitch black. You couldn't see a thing."

There was a shocked and awkward pause. Sue nodded, always eager to agree with Jen.

"But couldn't you, like, get raped? Plus everyone would hear you!" I said.

"Ew!" said Beth.

Jen rolled her eyes. "You guys are no fun. You had to be up for it, you know." She glanced at me. "Not everyone changes their mind after a kiss."

I glared back at her. *Grow up, Jen*!

Tania started to break the awkwardness by saying which bands she'd seen live that year. Sue showed us her new tattoo on her thigh of the word 'love'. Jen handed around red and white wine, gin and tonic and some fluorescent green homebrewed spirit that nobody would touch. Claire texted her new boyfriend on her phone.

There was a knock on the door and Jen sprung up. "That should be the boys."

"Boys?" I asked. "I thought it was just us girls?" Claire and Beth also looked surprised.

Jen laughed. "I invited them last minute. What would be the point in dressing up without boys to adore and admire us?" She tottered over to the door.

I quickly sat with my knees under me to make sure nobody

could see up my dress. My thoughts were tangled in Mike still. I wished people would stop bringing him up.

Beth touched me on the shoulder. "I've really got involved with acting in Uni; you guys should come watch a show sometime. Would be next year now, with exams this term."

I smiled. "I would love to. Text me some dates and I'll let you know."

"You been doing anything?" asked Claire. "I did trampolining for a bit and am now doing kung fu. I saw some pictures of you with a netball team?"

I nodded. "Yeah, I've been doing netball until recently." I paused. "I've actually been spending a lot of time looking at Christianity and thinking about morality and culture and things."

Beth and Claire raised their eyebrows. "Wow, sounds deep," said Claire.

I shrugged. "Not really. I just think it's important to decide what's true."

They both nodded. "We all need to think for ourselves. Good for you, Izzy," said Claire.

"Did it start because of Sarah?" asked Beth gently.

Suddenly the boys were coming into the room and we all got distracted. Mark came through first, who'd tried to chat me up at the river. Then to my horror was Tom, quickly followed by another rugby lad, John, and finally Will, who Jen had already latched onto. Each of them already had a beer in hand.

I couldn't help but fix my eyes on Tom. It was disturbing that even after everything that had happened, I still found him so attractive that my heartbeat increased and skin warmed when I looked at him. He looked even taller and broader than he had last year. He glanced at me and I looked away as quickly as I could, blushing. I hoped he would stay away from me, especially if Jen's mouth kept on spouting.

Mark sat down beside me and started asking questions about Uni. Jen gave me a full glass of red wine and I sipped it gratefully, hoping it would calm my nerves. I noticed Mark's eyes kept on slipping down my body as much as they had last year.

Jen clapped her hands and organised us into a card game. Every time you lost a point you had to take a shot of the toxic looking green liquor. Sue, who'd brought it, couldn't even say what flavour it was supposed to be or where exactly it had come from.

It turned out to be a game where you frequently lost points. The taste of the apple spirit mingled sourly with the taste of wine in my mouth. Then as people got knocked out of the game I found myself next to Tom. As I got progressively tipsy he just became more attractive. His hand brushed my knee and I smiled. I leant forward more than I needed to when I went to take a shot. Tom handed around cigarettes and I took one even though I knew Jen's parents would hate us smoking inside their house and I never ever smoked.

Mark drunkenly whispered, 'I think I'm getting drunk,' into my ear and I laughed. His arm wrapped around my waist and I pushed him off and smiled. He moved to put it around Sue's instead. Will and Jen were cuddling and kissing on the sofa. Beth and Claire were chatting happily in a corner and Tania was flirting with John even though I was sure neither was single.

It started to weirdly feel like Tom and I were on our own again. He put a hand on my shoulder. "I'm sorry about what happened last time, Izzy," he said. "I called you things I shouldn't have."

I smiled and shrugged off his apology, still avoiding his eyes. "I forgive you, it's cool. I shouldn't have given you mixed messages."

His hand found my chin and pulled my face to look at him. My whole body raced with the shock of his touch. "And what about the mixed messages you're giving me now, Izzy? What's going on in your head?" His gorgeous face was so close to mine... No! I wasn't going through this again. I needed to stop ignoring that small voice in my head telling me this was stupid and wrong. Tom didn't really care about me, I knew that. We just both found each other physically attractive but I'd already decided that wasn't the sort of relationship I wanted. He'd treated me horrifically before!

I stood up hurriedly and swayed. Great, I was drunk. "Sorry, Tom. I... I need to get home. I promised I wouldn't be late."

I quickly grabbed my heels from the floor and walked to the door without meeting anybody's eyes. Idiot! Absolute idiot!

I stood outside and dialled for a taxi. Then I walked around the corner so nobody in the house could see me standing on the street like a lemon instead of waiting inside. Hopefully the wind would take away some of the stink of smoke before I got home. My great-granny had died of lung cancer and my mum hated it if I even sat with smokers.

When the taxi finally arrived I bundled myself in. I realised that I should have asked if anyone wanted to share, but I was grateful to be alone. It was moments like this that I really felt like I needed Sarah. Why was I always so stupid with boys? Why couldn't I be attracted to a genuinely nice one, like Harry? One who didn't make me feel like it had to start with the pressures of sex? I half drunkenly dialled Fran's number and tried to control the sobs threatening to burst from the back of my throat.

Fran answered groggily and I realised it was late. Very late. "Hello? Everything all right, Izzy?"

"I've messed up, Fran. I got drunk and smoked and flirted with guys."

Fran paused down the phone as if mentally trying to catch up. I wondered if she was going to just try to get rid of me and go back to sleep. "You all right, Izzy? You home now?" She sounded genuinely concerned.

"I'm in a taxi. I'm fine. I just... do you think Jesus can forgive me for tonight?"

Another pause from Fran. "Jesus' blood washes away every sin, remember? But you have to accept His sacrifice first, Izzy," she said slowly. "If you can't accept that all the wrong you've done deserves recompense and that Jesus paid the price for you, then you're rejecting His forgiveness. You can't just want forgiveness for one event and ignore all the rest. It's like asking God if He can remove one grain of sand from a beach."

I just felt even more depressed. "But I feel like I owe God for this one. I'd made a sort of arrangement with Him. I was investigating Christianity to see if it was true. That meant trying to understand the way of living. I feel like God is showing me whether He's true or not and now I've broken my end of the deal."

"Izzy," said Fran gently. "It doesn't work like that. If God shows Himself to be true you need His forgiveness for everything. Only then can you have a clean slate. One that lasts forever. You can't try and live a perfect life without God's strength and help. Nobody can be perfect; it will destroy you."

I nodded to myself as the streetlights zipped over me. I think I sort of understood what Fran was saying but all my thoughts were sluggish and I was suddenly so tired.

"I'll call you in the morning, all right?" said Fran. "Get a good night's sleep, lovely."

She waited for my affirmation and then rang off. I felt slightly annoyed that she hadn't really answered my question. I let myself doze off until the taxi driver woke me.

*

The next day I was slightly hung over and Mum gave me a 'told you so' look. I hadn't even drunk *that* much. I texted Fran to apologise for the late night phone call and assured her she didn't need to call today, I was fine. I helped around the house and did the food shopping for the special dinner Mum wanted to cook. I even folded Jack's clothes after ironing even though he just screwed them up when he shoved them into his drawers or sport's bag. Whatever Fran had said, I felt like I needed to make up for last night, both to prove to God that I was serious, and to show Mum I was different than I had been before, despite what had happened.

I mulled over what I knew and about what Fran had said. Did I want to be forgiven for every stupid, hurtful and damaging thing I'd done? Yes. If that included being hurtful to God and damaging my relationship with Him by so actively ignoring Him all my life, I wanted to be forgiven for that too. I couldn't earn that forgiveness, just accept it. That was why it was 'amazing grace'. That was why not even the good rich man could get into Heaven by himself.

As I laid the table for Darren, I talked to God. First I explained what I was thinking, even though I guessed He'd probably heard most of my thoughts already which was a very strange thought. Then I said sorry. I said sorry for everything I'd ever done. I apologised for ignoring Him even when He'd given me Sarah. I apologised for all the times I'd lied and purposely hurt or ignored others. I apologised for being unfaithful to God, even though I was made by Him and promised to Him. Suddenly I was crying and had to rush upstairs before Mum could see. I wasn't used to apologising like this and being so humbled, it was scary and painful but at the same time, it felt like the right thing to do.

After I'd asked Jesus to forgive me for everything and I'd finally stopped crying, I waited. Nothing. No indication that He had heard. Nothing to show He accepted my apology. How did I know I was forgiven and accepted? I felt so lost all over again and slightly rejected. The doorbell made me jump as it sounded down stairs. I quickly re-did my make-up to hide the fact I'd been crying and went downstairs to meet Mum's new boyfriend. Maybe I just needed to be patient.

"Sanctify them by the Truth."

Chapter Fourteen

I came back to University a week early. I told Mum it was to start revision and finish some essays, but actually I just wanted to be back with friends and with nobody caring when I got up or went to bed. I wanted the feeling of control and freedom back. And no risk of Tom or Jen.

Holly had barely been at home at all. The medic exams were early and both Anna and she were buried under massive books and folders of paper. Even Anna was stressed now. After I'd unpacked I made them both cups of tea. Anna said she was worrying about putting too much of her identity into her exam results instead of Jesus. I didn't really understand what she meant by that but could see it concerned her so nodded and squeezed her shoulder then left them to it. I made a mental note to ask her after her exams were over. Chloe and Mike weren't back yet.

I settled into revision and reading bits of the Bible, writing notes of new things I learnt and of things I didn't understand in a notebook. Sometimes I didn't understand anything and just skipped it. I wished I was like Fran and understood it all so quickly and naturally. I was waiting for that dramatic click, when I would just get it.

The first day Fran was back I went to her flat and deliberately sneaked in, in case Josh was around. I felt like it would be too awkward to bump into him and didn't want him to think I was stalking him or something. His door was closed but the light was on. So he was back.

Fran was still unpacking so I made her bed for her while she unpacked her clothes and books. I'd never been in her room properly and asked about the people in her photos and the little stone elephants on her shelf. I realised our relationship was so focused on me I still barely knew her. And here I was to talk about me again. Was that selfish? Hopefully it would change more next year when we lived together. Maybe I should think of some way to show my appreciation to her at some point?

I settled on her bed once I'd finished tucking it in and pressed my back against the cool wall, hugging my knees. I felt like I was bursting with questions. "Fran, how do I know Jesus has forgiven me if I asked Him to?"

Fran stopped what she was doing in excitement and crawled onto the bed next to me. "You asked Jesus to forgive you for everything?"

I nodded. "But I listen for Him or look for a sign or feeling and He hasn't said He forgives me. I don't know if He accepts me."

Fran grabbed her Bible. "You know the Bible is the main way God speaks to us, right, Izzy? Well, this is what He is saying to you right now in answer to that question." She pointed to a verse in the Bible in a book called 1 John.

I read it out loud. "'If we say that we have no sin, we are deceiving ourselves and the truth is not in us. If we confess our sins, He is faithful and righteous to forgive us our sins and to cleanse us from all unrighteousness.'" I looked up at her. "So I'm forgiven?"

Fran nodded. "Anyone who genuinely confesses their sins to Jesus is forgiven. Look, Izzy, He has cleansed you of all unrighteousness."

I nodded. "And that definitely included me?"

Fran smiled. "Yes, Izzy, if you meant it and show you mean it. Jesus longs to forgive us, He died for us." She looked at me sideways. "You realise what this means?"

"What?"

"All you need to do is pledge to follow Jesus with your life, to honour Him, to show that you really are sorry and your repentance is genuine, and then you'll be a Christian. He'll look after you forever. Are you ready for that, Izzy?"

My heart started to thump in my chest. This was the moment I'd both been dreading and longing for. The moment to finally make a decision. It terrified me. "I don't know if I am quite ready, Fran," I said, panicked. "I want to be as thought through as I can be. I barely know my Bible. There's so much I don't understand. I still don't understand all that God wants from me."

Fran put her hand on my knee. "Izzy, being a Christian isn't about knowledge, though the Bible says we should seek it hungrily. But you have your whole life to learn about God. You know about Jesus' sacrifice and your sin. That is enough. You don't need any voices, or feelings or special permission from God. This is open to you whenever you feel you can sincerely commit to Him."

I nodded. "I'm almost ready. Just give me a few days, Fran. I feel like it just all needs to snap together in my mind."

I gave a half apologetic smile and left her room, wanting some time alone. However, I could hear voices in the flat as I fumbled with my keys at the door.

Mike had come back while I'd been with Fran. He gave me

his cursory nod as we passed between the bathroom and kitchen in the green emergency lights of the corridor. He didn't talk to me to make it clear the awkwardness wasn't over. I asked him how revision was going and he just grunted and shrugged.

I really felt like it was time this was all over. I sighed. "Mike, I am sorry about making it awkward in the flat and everything. I didn't mean to."

He held up his hands palms towards me and looked at me properly. "Hey, Izz, don't fret about it. It's cool. We can both move on now, hey? None of this relationship on hold business." He smiled and walked back into his room.

I turned back to the kitchen to turn on the kettle, not feeling appeased. Well I suppose I had just put our relationship on hold instead of properly ending it. Maybe I should tell Mike I didn't intend to ever resume it. Though I did still find him physically attractive. Maybe the fact that there was still a spark there was what made it so awkward between us. Maybe I needed to show him I had moved on? I mulled it over, slouched over the sideboard, tracing patterns in spilled sugar.

"Hey, Izzy, is there enough water in the kettle for me too?" It was Chloe's voice. I turned and gave her a big hug. She was still dressed for the outside and damp with rain.

"I thought you weren't coming back until Thursday." I topped up the kettle mid boil.

She shrugged, pulling off her coat. "Had a bit of an argument with my mum. It's my birthday tomorrow and I decided I wanted to spend it here rather than at home, even if people are being boring with revision." She nodded to the medics' doors. "Will you come out tonight, Izzy? Please? Help me celebrate in my nineteenth birthday? I'm sure we can find some people here who will join us. Will be like old times."

I nodded. Of course I would come out for her birthday. Especially as it was clear Anna and Holly couldn't. "Sounds good."

Chloe grinned, throwing her coat over a kitchen chair and taking the tea I offered her. "Thanks, babe. I'm going to ask Mike as well if you two can bear to be in the same room together?"

I smiled. "I think I can handle it, Chloe. Where are you wanting to go?"

She flopped down on the sofa and I joined her. "There's a 'shirts and short skirts' evening at Syndicate. Free entry if you put yourself on the guest list to arrive before ten." She flipped out her phone. "Aaaand you're on it."

"Don't most guys wear shirts and girl's short skirts clubbing anyway?" I asked. Sounded like the worse dress up code ever.

Chloe shrugged. "Suppose. I was going to wear a shirt knotted above my midriff and then a denim skirt, so gonna wear both."

I thought for a moment. "I don't own a shirt. I'll see if I can borrow one of Anna's though it might be the wrong size. I might borrow one of Mike's. Wear it loose over a strappy top or something?"

Chloe nodded. "Sounds good. I think Anna's shirts would be a bit tight in the breast department for you," she grinned. "Let me unpack and then we can get a few pre-drinks. I've invited a few course mates over."

*

Mike seemed very amused when I asked to borrow his shirt. He gave me his blue and white chequered one. It smelled of his aftershave and I thought it likely he'd not washed it since last wearing it. I realised with a jolt that it was what he'd been wearing when we had first slept together, but I didn't think he'd remember that. I'd also worn it once before, it and nothing else, when we'd just spent a morning lazing around his room. I'm sure he was more likely to remember that as he'd enjoyed looking at me. I wondered if he'd given me this shirt on purpose to remind me of that. Or it could have just been the one on the top of his drawer. I found the smell strangely reassuring. There had been times I'd been so happy with Mike. It was like time was going in a loop. Who was I now?

Chloe did my make-up for me and I did hers. We chatted about Easter holidays and plans for the summer, both deliberately avoiding the topic of exams.

First I put a crop top underneath the shirt, showing my tummy like Chloe, and almost as much cleavage. Then I hurriedly took it off, replacing it with a higher, and lower, strappy top. I was different now, remember? I didn't want to follow the hypocritical way of the culture around me. My identity wasn't in how beautiful or sexy I looked now. I didn't want to arouse men that looked at me, encouraging them to imagine sleeping with me. I wanted people to know me as a person. It had all made sense when it had come up in sermons and conversations with Christians, but it was hard now when I didn't want to be the odd one out, or appear the least attractive. I felt the urge to be loved by men more than by God.

I shook myself. "Come on, Izzy, it's just one party, not a moralistic dilemma on who you are," I muttered.

Just before we were ready to leave I went to Anna for peace of mind and twirled in my outfit. "Do you think it's appropriate?" I asked, feeling vulnerable. "Not too revealing?"

She smiled and kissed me on the cheek. "You look lovely." She winked. "Just don't bend over in that skirt."

I smiled. I'd learnt that rooky error years ago. I turned to go but Anna grabbed me. "Izzy, don't drink too much, right?" She seemed genuinely concerned. "I don't mean to mother you, but... it would be a shame if you threw away who you're becoming over a drunken incident."

I rolled my eyes. "Seriously, Anna, I'll be fine. I promised myself no boys at all until I know whether God exists and so what truly is the best way to do things."

She nodded. "I think you know whether God exists, Izzy. Don't ignore that fact when it doesn't suit and living the world's way seems too attractive." She gripped my arm. "Be strong."

I laughed at her. "You'd think I was going into battle, Anna. You want to come and chaperone me or something?"

She smiled to release the tension. "It is a battle, Izzy, and it doesn't take much to make or break somebody as on the edge as you."

I kissed her on the cheek back. "And you worry why normal people don't understand you lot." I gave her a wave. "See you later, alligator."

Anna nodded and got back to her revision.

*

I was squished in the middle of the taxi back seat between Mike and Chloe. A girl I didn't know sat in the front redoing her lipstick in the car mirror. I kept on waiting for the car to jolt or break suddenly and make her draw red across her face, but the taxi driver clearly didn't have enough of a sense of humour. I'd only drunk a Coke in pre-drinks but accepted a shot of vodka and Coke from Chloe in the back. I felt uncomfortable being right next to Mike again, especially after how weak I'd been with Tom in the holidays. That rush of emotions when a good looking guy was close was just so powerful.

Once we reached the club I made sure I didn't drink anything but water. It was actually easier than I thought it would be since nobody offered to buy me anything, and nobody was taking any notice of what I was having. As I looked around me without alcohol affecting my perception everything seemed different. The music was too loud to talk. Everywhere people were kissing and groping each other. The toilets were full of drunken girls sitting on the floor or vomiting or crying into another's arms. The songs were extremely suggestive. Everything seemed to be about sex. Cheap sex with no consequences or meaning.

I enjoyed dancing for the first thirty minutes but then everything started to become repetitive and stressful. With the rest of the party so drunk, it made me feel like I should be watching out for them, making sure nobody got lost or taken home by somebody suspicious. I was so much more tired than I had been in a club before. I started to feel like Esther must have done. She must have felt so alone in a culture obsessed with money and beauty and alcohol and excess. It was so clear that in this club, those things were worshiped above all else. She must have felt so small and out of place, yet God had been there, even when He'd never been mentioned. He had been there even though there hadn't been any in-your-face miracles. He'd been there even when she'd been the only believer in the whole court. And He had saved her and His people.

I believed in God, I knew that now. After everything I'd seen and heard I just couldn't deny that fact. My problem was how did I respond to that? How did I respond to Jesus' dying two thousand years ago so I could be forgiven? Could I admit how much trouble I was in without Him? When culture around me seemed to think nothing was wrong or right apart from the extremities of murder, stealing or rape. Did I really want to be part of this world? Or the future perfect one which was coming? The one with no death, suffering or confusion. The one Sarah and Esther had lived for.

Alone at the edge of the dance floor, I let God know I was ready. "Thank you, Jesus for dying for me," I said out loud. "Thank you for forgiving me for the mess I've made with my life. I'm ready to follow you now. I know your way is best. I know I can't earn your forgiveness or pay you back. But I will do my best to live a life which honours you."

I suddenly felt much lighter. The burden of months of thought and confusion suddenly lifted. My perception of everything stopped flipping from wildly different perspectives and was fixed. I'd made my choice and now the world was starting to make more sense. I needed to tell Fran and Anna. They would be so happy.

I pushed through the crowd in search of Chloe, but one of her course mates said she had already left with a guy from their year. Apparently they'd been 'on and off' for a while now so I had nothing to worry about. Instead I went in search of Mike. He was less drunk than I had feared, and to my surprise, agreed he was happy to leave. He had a friend with him who lived at the top of Whiteladies and had driven in. He offered us a lift. Once I'd determined that he was sober, I accepted. As we walked outside, the sudden cold was shocking and our breath misted. We walked slowly to the car due to my heels and the friend introduced himself as Simon.

"I wanted to leave early, anyway," he said. "Clubbing's so much less fun when you're sober and I have a job interview tomorrow so didn't want to be home late or hung over." He looked a few years older than us and I wondered if he was finishing a masters. My mind was buzzing with so many new ideas and realisations, now I followed Jesus, that I couldn't concentrate enough to make normal conversation. How silly that he felt he needed to give an excuse as to why he wasn't drunk to a stranger. It was crazy, yet that had been me four months ago. How had I let all of that stuff have such a hold over me? It felt so freeing to realise I didn't have to care how cool or beautiful anyone thought I was. That was so far away from what life was really about.

Mike said to Simon it was fine to drop us off outside his house, we could walk the last ten minutes across the Down's on our own. I hesitated when he said this. It was so cold out there I'd been hoping to be dropped off in Durdham carpark, especially since I couldn't walk quickly in heels. But I didn't know Simon and he was doing us a favour, so I didn't say anything.

We got out of the car on one of the tiny, steep, twisting roads off the top of Whiteladies. Mike slapped Simon on the back, and then we started to trudge towards the Downs, using the more direct, little windy roads. Mike clearly had something on his mind as well and kept quiet. He wasn't very steady on his feet with the uneven flagstones and I realised he had been hiding how drunk he actually was from Simon. I wondered if he was still ignoring me. We reached the top of the hill and the start of the Downs. Instead of walking along the pavement to the well-lit road that split the Down's in two, Mike decided to take a more direct route and took off diagonally across the grass. I was going to argue, but then it really was cold. Even if the mud ruined my shoes, at least we'd be back quickly.

The moon was bright above us and there was a strange mist seeping out of the grass around us, giving everything a ghostly beauty. There was barely any traffic noise and everything took on a magical, surreal quality. I thanked God for the beauty of His creation.

Mike cleared his voice next to be, making me jump. He had clearly slowed down his walk so I could keep up. "What really happened between us, Izzy?" I was completely taken aback by his question.

"What do you mean? I didn't feel like I could go out with you after you kissed that girl."

Mike frowned down at the floor. "Was that really the only reason, or was it an excuse? You were acting more and more withdrawn towards the end. And when you did put things on pause, I thought you were probably going to forgive me."

I shrugged. "Well you moved on pretty fast. You didn't seem to regret our break up."

Mike sighed. "I was trying to give you space."

I shrugged again. I had no idea if he was telling the truth or not, but he was certainly a womaniser and I didn't want to be played with any more. From now on my relationships were going to be special and mean something, and that really excited me. I was going to look for a guy who would treat me with the dramatic self-sacrificial love and high honour the Bible demanded of husbands. A guy I could feel safe to respect and lead me in my faith. Somebody who could teach me more about Jesus. Wouldn't it be amazing to have both our lives based on the same thing? Both in love with Jesus. Both with the same opinions on morality and money and family.

Mike stopped to face me and I realised I had completely zoned out of our conversation. All around us the mist was rising now, gilding the air with moonlight. I was shivering and Mike put his hands on my arms as if to warm me. He stepped close. "Do you miss it, Izzy? Do you miss our relationship? 'Cos I miss you."

I took a step back, my mind sharply coming into focus. "Mike…"

"Do you remember our second date, here on the Downs?" He flung an arm out to our dark and empty surrounds. "We kissed for hours remember? You were so nervous at first but gained confidence fast. And every time I leaned close your breath sped up." He stepped close again and it suddenly hit home how alone we were. There was nobody who could see us and possibly nobody within earshot either. That should have terrified me, but I felt strangely calm.

I put a hand on his chest and pushed him away gently. "I don't want that any more, Mike. I'm sorry."

He put his hand over mine. "Just one more night, Izzy. You'll be in control and then we can see. It will be like good old times." He tugged at his shirt with its ends tied under my chest. "The most beautiful you've ever looked was when you only wore this shirt. Do you remember? You have an incredible body, Izzy." He leaned his face towards mine.

I pushed his hand away from my clothes and started to walk away. "No, Mike! Listen to me! I don't want you. I don't care if you're desperate for sex tonight, I'm not interested."

"Izzy!" I felt him try to grab me from behind. The warmth of his breath tingled my freezing skin. The alcohol stung my nose. "We were good together."

I turned and shoved him as hard as I could. He was caught off balance and fell over into the wet grass. The mist flew out from around him. "Go away, Mike!" I said.

Mike got up and wiped his face on his sleeve. I could tell he was really angry now I'd pushed him over. His face was twisted with wounded pride. "Fine! Whatever!"

And he went away, running across the Downs, the mist closing behind him. At last, a proper closure with Mike. At last I knew what I was doing.

I tried to follow in the direction that Mike had run in, but the mist was higher than my head now and I could only just make out the bright outline of the moon. I suddenly wasn't sure if I was still walking in the right direction. I muttered a prayer to God for Him to help me get home. I untied Mike's shirt and used it to wrap around me better.

I walked a few wobbling steps further and looked around. It was pitch black though the mist and shadows moved everywhere. I couldn't even hear any traffic to walk towards. My heels were sinking into the mud so I pulled them off and walked bare foot. The wet grass was starting to crystallise with frost. Common sense told me I needed to be able to run fast if I had to, alone out here on the Downs. But I still couldn't feel afraid.

I walked forward, completely disorientated and jumped as a branch from a bush brushed my arm. I stood still for a few minutes to see if anyone was hiding behind it, then sighed and got out my phone. This was ridiculous. I needed help, I knew I did. I wasn't safe, even if I couldn't let the reality of it hit me. I needed somebody to get me home. I had asked for God to help me and somehow I knew He was. He was with me right now. He could be my strength and protector whatever happened. I was nestled, enveloped in Him.

I pulled Mike's shirt tighter around me and tried to stop myself shivering. I just wanted my lovely warm bed where I could finally sleep. I scrolled through my contacts and almost called Anna or Fran but then thought it would be even worse to have them wandering around the Downs gone midnight, alone. So I couldn't really phone anyone but Josh, could I?

My hands were tied whether he liked me talking to him or not.

I pressed his number and jiggled up and down, the cold seeping through my tights and up my legs. It was hard to move my toes and fingers now. Come on... pick up!

"Hello, Izzy?" came Josh's quiet voice. He sounded groggy from sleep. I really needed to stop calling people after they'd gone to bed. "You all right?"

"Sorry to wake you, Josh, but I need a little bit of help." I took a deep breath. "You see I'm on my own on the Downs since Mike ran off and I'm a bit lost and cold."

There was the sound of hurried activity down the phone. "Don't worry; I'm coming to get you. Any idea where you are?"

It seemed strange to hear Josh's deeply concerned voice contrasting with my own nonchalant tone. "I'm on the half closest to the gorge by a bush. I crossed Lady's Mile about a minute ago but can't find it now."

"Okay. I'm going to get Fran and some others and we'll be right there." More noise and clatter. "You sound very calm, Izzy."

"I know; I just can't feel scared. Just cold." I realised that sounded worrying. "Oh, don't worry, Josh, not in a hypothermia sort of way. I think I'm fine. You see, you don't need to worry about me anymore. I've become a Christian."

"You have?"

"Yeah, it's one of the reasons I rang you. You see you can be around me again now."

"Izzy, that's hardly a reason *not* to ring me when you're lost on..."

"Yeah, I know, I know, but, like, it's just so exciting, isn't it? God's my dad now. I finally have a perfect dad. And even if somebody murders me out here, I get to go to Heaven and then the perfect future on Earth made new. And only stuff can happen within God's plan, right? I dunno I just feel so peaceful now. And happy. But cold."

"Izzy, that's great, but nobody's going to murder you, I promise. Just keep warm, we're coming. I need to ring off now, but I'll ring again in a few minutes. Just keep warm and hide if you see anyone suspicious. I can't believe Mike left you out there! The idiot."

"Okay, will do. Thanks, Josh."

I stuffed my hands under my armpits and started to pace in little circles. I wanted to sit down but was worried the wet grass would just make me colder. I had always felt a hole in who I was and who I was supposed to be after Dad ran off to America. I was supposed to be half him genetically, but I'd never wanted to be like him in any way. Now I had a new dad. I could be like Him instead. And He would love and look after me perfectly.

I started muttering a prayer under my breath. "Thank you, God, that I can be yours after how long I've rejected and ignored you. Thank you now that you're my protector and dad. Please help them find me quickly, because I really am cold now. Thanks for protecting me from Mike. Thank you for not letting me be scared. You're so kind to me. Thank you for giving me Fran and Anna and Josh in Halls. I assume they've been constantly asking you things to do with me. That you would rescue me and stuff. Well, thanks for answering their prayers. And, well, I don't know what else Josh has been asking about me. I assume it's cheating for anyone to ask you for me to become their girlfriend? Oh I don't know. But he is quite sweet. Well, anyway thank you that he picked up and is coming."

A branch snapped behind me and I jumped. Silence. Then

another crack. I couldn't see a thing. I squatted under the bush and asked God if He could make them go away if they meant harm. There were so many stories of what had happened to people on the Downs... My phone vibrated in my hand but I didn't answer so that my voice and the light wouldn't give me away. I waited. My phone vibrated again. No more snaps of twigs. But I hadn't heard anyone or anything leave. Were they still there? My legs were becoming so cold I worried I wouldn't be able to stand and run in a hurry without them cramping. I kept still and watched my breath mist become part of the fog. I remembered the first few lines of the Psalm that Anna had above her bed. *'The Lord's my shepherd, I shall not want. He makes me lie in green pastures, he leads me beside still waters. His goodness restores my soul.'* He was there shepherding me. Looking after me. Therefore, I wanted for nothing. I strained to hear footsteps.

Suddenly I heard distant voices. People shouting my name. I waited a few more minutes, waiting for them to startle off whoever was there. If anyone had ever been there. The shouts were coming closer. Slowly I stood up, gritting my teeth as my cold muscles complained. There was no sound around me so I took a few steps towards the voices. Still no sound from behind, so I yelled back as loud as I could, and started to wander towards the noise.

A torch suddenly made the mist flash in front of me in dancing swirls. I called again. Then a shadow was running towards me that became Josh. He ran to wrap me in a tight embrace. Pressed against his chest I thought it was a bit inappropriate compared to his normal cautious behaviour, but thought it was wise not to tell him off after he'd come out here to rescue me. Besides, it felt quite nice and his heart was racing. Probably just because he'd been running.

"It's all right, we're here," he whispered into my hair. Then we parted and he wrapped his coat around me. He wasn't even wearing a jumper and I noticed he was wearing pyjama bottoms and flip-flops. He must have rushed out of his room without thinking. "Oh, Izzy, you're frozen. Come on, let's get you back."

He shouted into the mist and Anna, Fran, Holly and two of Josh's flatmates appeared, all looking worried. They all hugged me and made comments on how cold I was and pale I looked. I couldn't really understand what all the fuss was about and just wanted to tell Anna and Fran about becoming a Christian.

Halfway back I suddenly felt very sleepy and weak. I barely noticed Josh and Fran pick me up to carry me home, and could only mumble when Fran tucked me in with a hot water bottle and promised to stay with me all night. I vaguely realised I'd left my shoes on the Downs somewhere, but couldn't formulate the words.

*

The next morning Mike came in to apologise for his behaviour and leaving me, blaming it on the drink. I told him I forgave him, but that he was as responsible for his drunken actions as his non drunken ones and that therefore he probably shouldn't get drunk anymore. Mike had been too embarrassed to retort. I spent the day on my bed reading and sleeping. I'd never felt so exhausted in my life. However, the next morning I just felt like I couldn't keep God to myself any more. He'd saved me! He loved me! He was real! Everyone just had to hear about this.

I wrote in my Bible words to match Sarah's, '*Your cross*

changes everything'. I sat looking at it excitedly and thought about all the different ways that saying was true and who I could convey that same message to.

I sat excitedly waiting for Mum to pick up the phone. One ring. Two. Three. "Hello?"

"Mum! Hi, it's Izzy."

"Izzy! Darling! Lovely to hear your voice. You've not replied to any of my texts about your exam dates, I was beginning to wonder if you'd turned into some sort of recluse."

"Sorry, Mum, I've been doing a lot of thinking and guess what I found out? Christianity is true! Like, God and Jesus and the Holy Spirit are real. I thought it was something just for people who wanted to be 'spiritual' but it's actually objectively true!"

There was silence down the other end of the phone. I just needed to tell her the same things I'd heard and then she'd realise it was true too. It was just a lack of information; it seemed so obvious now I had it all before me.

"Are you having me on, Izzy?"

"No, Mum. I'm being more serious than I ever have been in my life, it's just so exciting! I'm so happy!"

"Eh, ok, well... does this mean you're going to go to church and stuff?"

"I'm already going with a friend. Remember I have a flatmate called Anna? You know, Mum, it was nothing like I expected it to be. Each sermon is about day to day life and what the Bible says about it. Did you know the Bible speaks into, like, every area and it's just so perceptive? Mum, you've got to read it!"

"Wow, Izzy," Mum said calmly. "I've not heard you this hyped up for ages. Well, what else is going on? You going to tell me when those exams are? Do any count for next year?"

"But, Mum, don't you want to hear more about Christianity? Don't you see how it affects everyone if it's true? How important it is?"

"Now, Izzy," said Mum more firmly. "It's fine for you to believe whatever you want but you can't start forcing others around you to think the same way."

"Mum, I'm not forcing you, I just want you to see how relevant it is, how much Jesus has done for you."

"Izzy, I really don't need that stuff in my life right now. If God is real he's given me an awful load of crap to be good and all that."

"That's what I used to think, but actually He's done us so much good by dying for us. And yes you do need Him, Mum. Everyone does. You see you've been unfaithful to him so deserve to go to Hell and need to be rescued like I have."

"I think that's quite enough, Isabelle. I know you're still upset about Sarah but you can't talk to me like that. You can ring me again when you're feeling more sensible and considerate."

She hung up.

I paused in shock. I had thought she'd want to know and really listen to what had happened to me. I thought she'd become a Christian too as soon as I'd explained. I suddenly felt very hurt at the sudden distance between us. I hurried to Anna's room and relayed our conversation.

Anna listened quietly and then made us both a cup of tea so I had time to calm down. It reminded me of Sarah's hot chocolates and I smiled to myself. We'd have those together again one day. There *had* to be hot chocolate in Heaven.

Anna, as always, thought carefully about what she was going to say before she started. "I know this is all new to you, Izzy, and exciting, and that is really good. But you need to remember this is a very sensitive issue and unique to every person. If people just needed to hear a set number of things to become a Christian, we would have landed on the formula years ago and most people would be Christians. It's not just logic; the Holy Spirit needs to soften people's hearts in order for them to become a Christian. In short, it's a miracle. I know you feel you just need to tell people and they'll see it, but that's just not true. You need to be very sensitive and go slowly." She paused to sip her tea, studying my face to make sure I wasn't crying. "There's a verse in the Bible somewhere..." She flicked to the concordance in the back, muttering that she wished she knew it as well as Fran. "It's here somewhere," she said sheepishly, giving up. "Well it says what I just said."

"I just really thought she'd be hungry to hear everything. I assumed she'd just thought Christianity was not true but if I'd become a Christian she'd be really curious."

Anna smiled and held my hands. "And I'm sure she will become more and more curious as she sees how much it's changed you. But you need to be sensitive. This is an area where it's very easy for two people to hear completely different things."

I nodded. "What should I do?"

Anna sighed. "I think you should apologise to your, mum, and then perhaps wait until she's willing to talk about it again. Subtly bring it into conversations. Show her how much it means to you. Love her. Work out what barriers are between her and the Gospel. But most of all pray for her. Without God, she's not going to be saved."

I nodded. "I should have prayed before calling her, shouldn't I?"

Anna was doing her thinking pause again. "Also, Jesus said we would face much rejection and persecution for becoming

Christians. He said that following Him would tear up families. You need to be prepared for that."

I nodded but was still too shocked for the full meaning of her words to sink in. This was already harder than I thought it was. But if Jesus had sweat tears of blood for me and my mum, I could persevere for my mum.

*

The next few days I spent trying to think through everything I'd learned which was so different from what I'd been taught before. I tried to see how it would affect every context of my life. I tried to tell a few people about what had happened to me, but nobody was interested. People who'd thought it was good for me to look into Christianity and faith suddenly didn't want to talk about it now I actually thought it was true. Church became such a haven.

It was funny that suddenly these people understood me more than my old friends and own family. And in many ways they started to surround me and look out for me as a new family who genuinely cared. They asked personal questions about my wellbeing; gave me lifts and fed me countless meals on Sundays. I also started to feel really excited about Hall CU. Fran and Josh had handed down leadership to the first years and Anna, Joel and Mei were nervously taking up the mantle. Every week I threw dozens of questions at them, in and after every Bible study.

A week later and I still hadn't managed to have a proper conversation with Mum about Christianity. I lay on my bed with my forehead rested on the revision I should have been doing and decided I should give up trying to work and go and unload on Fran. I hoped the exam 'fear' would grab me soon and help me to actually work, or I was going to fail these exams so badly. Then I remembered that I could pray about that, so added it to my list to pray later.

I knocked on Fran's flat's door and waited for somebody to open it. To my surprise it was Josh. I stupidly felt myself blush in surprise and hurriedly looked away to hide it. Then I realised that almost looked worse, so met his eyes. They really were nice eyes.

"Hi," I ventured, trying to remember why I'd gone there. "Is Fran in?"

"Yes," he said. He opened the door wider, so I could see in, but didn't move back. He hesitated. His eyes flickered to my lips for the briefest of seconds.

"You going to let me in then, Josh?" I asked, half smiling, taking a step forward.

"Yes, yes, of course. I… I was just wondering…" He didn't move and we were suddenly closer than I'd intended.

"Yes?"

"Would you like to go out for a coffee sometime, Izzy?"

Fran's grinning head popped out horizontally from her door behind Josh. She was mouthing '*A date! A date! That's 'Christian' for a date!*' Then she disappeared and I was alone again with Josh. He noticed where I was looking and looked behind himself in confusion.

I tried to remove Fran from my mind. My heart was suddenly racing and my mouth was dry. I needed to be sensible. And, as strange as the thought was, I needed to prioritise God. I really, really liked Josh, but right now I needed to get other things straight. For the first time in years I realised I didn't actually need a boyfriend. I wasn't 'missing out' if I didn't have one. I was already loved and treasured.

"Josh," I started, awkwardly, keeping my eyes away from

his face. "For years now I've rotated my life around boys and potential relationships. I was wondering if you could give me time to work out how to rotate my life around God instead, and my relationship with Him? Then, maybe next term or so, I can, eh... be in a relationship without making it the be all and end all." I dared a glance up at him. "Does that make sense? I'm sorry."

Josh quickly held up his hands. "Not at all, Izzy, I'm sorry for asking so quickly. I'll give you all the space you need."

"Hey," I smiled gently, touching his shoulder. "I'd love to just be friends first. Brother and sister as Christians. Family."

Josh grinned. "We'll always be family, Izzy, for eternity now."

I smiled and paused awkwardly. Josh didn't move. "Well, will you let me in now?"

Josh quickly removed his hand from the door and stepped out of my way. "Of course, sorry. You two have a nice time." He moved quickly into his room.

I walked to Fran's room. She was sat still on her bed with a quiet smile on her face, watching me. "That was a very brave decision, Izzy, I'm so proud of you."

I shrugged in embarrassment. "I'm just not sure I'm ready for a relationship as a Christian yet. I've always put far too much expectation on them. Boys have always been my biggest temptation. I want to see that Jesus is more important. Also, I don't want to fall into the trap of thinking all Christian boys are perfect and will make great boyfriends. I picked bad men before, I know I did, it wasn't just that they were not Christians. I know plenty of 'nice' non-Christians. I just... I just need to work it all out in my head rather than using Christianity as a tool to get nicer boys. I don't know. Did that make any sense at all?"

Fran nodded and smiled, putting an arm around me and pulling me onto the bed. Then she grinned. "You know I only see Josh that nervous and awkward when he's talking to you."

I hit her with her pillow. "Stop it, Fran," I smiled back. "I came here to talk about Christian stuff, not boys."

She leaned over to grab her Bible and smiled at me in a more sensible manner. I tried to get Josh out of my head so I could talk about the things I was struggling with. "I suppose, I'm trying to learn as much as I can as fast as I can, but it's all a bit overwhelming and Jesus still feels quite distant. I just feel so far away from being a proper Christian. And I tell people the facts and the evidence and they don't want to listen or become Christians."

Fran nodded and started flicking through her Bible, squeezing my hand. "It's not all about logic, Izzy. Christianity isn't purely a bunch of facts. It's not *just* about the way you live your life, the way you treat other people and the fact you read your Bible every day. That's just religion. You need to engage your heart as well; you need to let yourself be changed."

I tried to dissect her words feeling overwhelmed by all I'd stumbled into. I felt like a child again. But this new world felt so fresh and exciting, I wanted to understand every last bit. "You mean remember how much Jesus loves me and that He died for me?"

"Yes but more than that. You need to realise the intimate relationship that you have with God and feel and act on it in every area of life. You *are* close to Jesus, that's a fact, even when you don't feel like it. Look at Romans 8:15, '*For you did not receive a spirit that makes you a slave again to fear, but you received the Spirit of sonship. And to him we cry, "Abba," Father.*' When you become a Christian you become God's child, His heir. You are close enough to God to call Him

'Daddy', that's what 'Abba' means." She flicked through her Bible to John 1: 12-13. "'*But to all who did receive him, who believed in his name, he gave the right to become children of God, who were born, not of blood nor of the will of the flesh nor of the will of man, but of God.*' Isn't that incredible? We're His children, that makes us so close to Him! And also the church is Christ's bride. Can you think of two more intimate relationships than that of parent and child, husband and wife? That is the relationship you already have with God from the moment you gave your life to follow Him. We were created for this relationship; it fulfils everything, even our deepest needs. It's the answer to loneliness, self-image, peer pressure, bad habits, and unrealistic relationships with others. God can be our everything. He is with us every day, every second. We can talk to Him constantly, share all our worries and burdens, learn about His heart for others. He wrote us a whole book to help us discover Him and He has so much to communicate with us. He loves us even when we don't love Him. Remember His awesomeness every day, Izzy. Remember His power. He created everything. He is in control of everything. You have nobody else to fear. And He can be the most intimate relationship you have, your closest friend." She paused and smiled and stroked my hair behind my ear. "Don't miss out, Izzy. I missed out on this for years, even as a Christian, when I just treated it as a set of rules. God doesn't fit in a box. Life will be hard and complicated on Earth. Explore God and your relationship with Him, run your race to the end no matter what sufferings come your way. Let others see Christ in you as you live your life for Him, and then enjoy it in perfection for eternity."

*

I got back to my room sieved through the richness of Fran's words and prayed to God about everything that was on my mind from the day. I decided I needed to pray to Him throughout the day, remembering He was with me constantly. Like the way I had constantly chatted and unloaded to Sarah. I paused, thinking about her. There was one thing I'd never been able to do. Read the last page of Sarah's diary and see what had been on her mind just before her death. Now I didn't feel intimidated by it anymore. Death was a monster that shouldn't be here but Jesus had defeated it and one day there would be no more death. We would be united again. I smiled thinking how happy she would be to find me a Christian. All the friction in our relationship, gone.

I reached under my bed and pulled out her diary. I opened to the last page and took a deep breath before reading.

'Dear God,

I lost my temper with Izzy last night, I'm so sorry. It just makes me so angry what happened between her and Tom. I'm so worried she's going to end up in a destructive relationship. But I was sinful and there is no excuse for that. I'm so sorry; please help me be more gracious to her in the future.

I found the whole evening so hard. When she kept on trying to get me clubbing or drunk or dating, even though she knows I don't want to. She always gets so defensive towards me before clubbing. Either she feels deep down that she's doing something wrong, or she feels like I'm judging her, even when I don't say a thing. I find it so hard to keep neutral and not get annoyed at her. Tonight it just all came out. Father, she never lets me talk about you, and it feels like she can't accept the most important thing about me. I care about her so deeply, yet she doesn't have the most crucial thing in life. I find myself thinking that she can never be saved, she's so far away. But I know you are almighty and all powerful. I know you are in complete control. So please save her. If not through me, then through somebody else. Even if it destroys our relationship, let me never give up.

But, Father, whatever your plans are for my friends, use me in whatever way to bring you glory. Any suffering in this life is only momentary and in the face of joy for eternity. It makes me so happy to remember the future you have bought for me.

Thank you that I can always rely on your strength. I pray that one day Izzy will too.

Amen.'

'He will wipe every tear from their eyes. There will be no more death or mourning or crying or pain, the old order of things has passed away.'

Revelation 21:4

Lightning Source UK Ltd.
Milton Keynes UK
UKHW010628060421
381519UK00001B/247